By Riley Brooks

SCHOLASTIC INC.
New York   Toronto   London   Auckland
Sydney   Mexico City   New Delhi   Hong Kong

No part of this publication may be reproduced in whole or in part, stored in
a retrieval system, or transmitted in any form or by any means, electronic,
mechanical, photocopying, recording, or otherwise, without written
permission of the publisher. For information regarding permission, write to
Scholastic Inc., Attention: Permissions Department, 557 Broadway,
New York, NY 10012.

© 2009 by Scholastic

ISBN-13: 978-0-545-19657-4
ISBN-10: 0-545-19657-4

Published by Scholastic Inc.
SCHOLASTIC and associated logos are trademarks and/or registered
trademarks of Scholastic Inc.

12 11 10 9 8 7 6 5 4 3 2 1   9 10 11 12 13 14/0

Designed by Deena Fleming
Printed in the U.S.A.
First printing, August 2009

CONTENTS:

INTRODUCTION

Before they went onstage, the cast of the popular Disney show *Wizards of Waverly Place* gathered together in a close circle to say a prayer and have a cheer and pep talk. "We check our teeth, our hair, you can hear the audience is right there [cheering and clapping]," Selena Gomez told DisneySociety.com. "We gather around with our producers and make sure we say a good prayer because we would not be here if it weren't for all the audience and for God . . ." Then it was time for the taping to begin. Selena Gomez, who stars as Alex on the show, was transformed as soon as the lights came up. Before filming began, she was a normal laid-back teenager, but once the cameras were on, she stole the show. The audience couldn't look away as Selena delivered her lines and cracked jokes with her co-stars. She completely drew the audience into the story.

In that day's episode, Alex was about to turn fifteen and her parents had planned her an elaborate quinceañera to celebrate. In Hispanic cultures, the quinceañera is a traditional Latin American celebration marking a girl's fifteenth birthday and her transition from girlhood to womanhood. But Alex isn't excited about dressing up and going through all of the rituals until her grandmother explains how important these family traditions are. Alex's mom always wanted to have a fancy quinceañera but her family couldn't afford it. So Alex uses her wizard powers to swap bodies with her mom. That way her mom gets to have the quinceañera she's always wanted. Alex's mom loves the party, and the two switch back toward the end. Alex returns to her own body just in time for a traditional dance with her father. Dancing with her dad and hearing him tell her how proud he is of the young woman she has become, Alex realizes just how important her cultural traditions are.

The audience laughed at every joke and a few viewers even got misty-eyed as Alex and her dad shared their special dance. Peter Murrieta, one of the show's executive producers and writers, was front and center watching the performance. "I think that working on this show, seeing the depths and the abilities these actors have shown me, I really believe that they can evolve," he told the *Fort Worth Star-Telegram*. "The sky's the limit. I wouldn't at all be surprised to see them having careers in film or TV. They're incredibly talented, and they have a passion."

It was a touching episode, and one of Selena's favorites to film. Selena's father is from Mexico and she was brought up with many of the Hispanic traditions featured on the show. Selena was very excited to show off her culture to viewers who might not know anything about Hispanic families. In fact, Selena has been very vocal about her heritage and how important it is to her. "I didn't even realize what a big deal it was to be Latin at first. But then one day being with my dad, it hit me: it's pretty neat to be Mexican. And there aren't enough Latinas in Hollywood — or there are, but they don't get the recognition. So to be able to come out here and use that, it's really a powerful thing," Selena explained to *Latina*. Selena is a role model to kids from all different backgrounds, but she's especially proud to give other Latina girls someone to look up to. She never imagined she'd get the chance to influence so many fans when she went to her very first Disney casting call only a few years before.

Since she caught the attention of Disney, Selena has moved to Hollywood, made *Wizards of Waverly Place* one of the most popular shows in Disney history, and earned herself thousands of fans. Her show was in its second season and Selena couldn't have been happier! Of course, she didn't know then just how much bigger and better her career was about to become. Selena's star is still on the rise, and there is really no limit to just how far she'll go!

CHAPTER 1:
Texas Sweetheart

It was a beautiful summer day when Mandy and Ricardo Gomez welcomed their beautiful baby girl, Selena Marie Gomez, into the world on July 22, 1992. She was born in a New York City hospital. Her young parents were so thrilled with their newborn that they wanted to give her a name that she could carry proudly. They named her Selena Marie Gomez, after one of their favorite Mexican singers, superstar Selena Quintanilla-Perez.

Selena Quintanilla-Perez was one of the most talented and best loved Mexican-American singers in history. Selena recorded eleven albums and won many music awards. She was also the first woman to earn a gold record in Tejano music, a very well known style of Mexican folk music. Sadly, Selena Perez was murdered by her fan club president in 1995, just after finishing her first English crossover album. Her death was a tragic loss. Even today, dedicated Selena fans still journey to Corpus Christie, Texas, to pay their respects at her grave. Selena Gomez really enjoys Selena Quintanilla-Perez's music, and visited her grave with her father when she was a little girl. Selena Gomez has always felt honored to share her name with the famous Tejano star.

Ricardo Gomez, Selena's father, was from Guadalajara, Mexico, a beautiful area considered to be a hotbed for musical talent in Mexico. Selena's mother, Amanda "Mandy" Cornett Gomez was an actress from Dallas, Texas. When Selena was born, the young family was in New York City temporarily working in the theater community there. They loved their precious baby girl more and more as she grew up. With her big, brown eyes, thick dark brown hair, and creamy olive skin, Selena was an absolutely adorable toddler. Unfortunately, life was hard for the Gomez family in New York City. Mandy and Ricardo had married very young and money was tight. They moved to Grand Prairie, Texas, to be closer to family when Selena was just a toddler. Mandy had grown up in Texas, and Selena loved being closer to her grandmother and cousins. Sadly, the move to Texas couldn't fix Mandy and Ricardo's marriage. They loved each other and Selena, but they found themselves fighting often. Finally, they made the tough decision to get a divorce. Selena was only five years old. "There were a lot of tears," Selena confessed to M magazine. The divorce was hard for Selena, but she has remained close to both of her parents.

Selena lived with Mandy, and even though she missed living with her father, Selena was glad that both her parents were happy. Eventually Mandy remarried Brian Teefey from Michigan. Selena got along well with her stepfather right away and she was very excited to see her mother so happy. ". . . I have a stepdad. And honestly, I love him with all my heart. I see how happy my mom is with him, which is awesome," Selena told M magazine.

Selena spent lots of time with her father's family as well as her mother's. She's very proud of their shared Hispanic heritage. Selena told *Scholastic News* about her family traditions. "My family does have quinceñaras, and we go to the communion church. We do everything that's Catholic, but we don't really have anything traditional except go to the park and have barbecues on Sundays after church."

Selena loved growing up in Texas. She had both sides of the family nearby so she was never without plenty of love and support. "I've had the same friends since kindergarten, so everyone is still really close. And I'm really close to all my family — my cousins, my aunts, my grandmother and grandpa," Selena told *Girls' Life Magazine*. With the support of her family, Selena grew into an adorable tomboy who was always playing outside. She made friends with all of the kids in her neighborhood, but especially the boys.

Selena and her friends, guys and girls, always had a lot of fun hanging out together. "We live in the nice suburb areas, and everybody knows everybody in that little neighborhood. We could all walk outside and hang out. . . . We used to walk around the blocks a lot . . . but other than that it's pretty normal. You can go to skate parks, or you can go to the mall or movies with your friends," Selena explained to *Girls' Life Magazine* about her hometown. The boys may not have been into girly things, but they did teach Selena a lot about sports, and basketball is her favorite. She began playing when she was young, and even played on her school team for a while. "I used to be on a team for school, and then I got homeschooled, so not anymore. . . . I'm a huge basketball fan. My favorite [team] is the San Antonio Spurs. . . . Back home, all my guy friends were Dallas Mavericks fans so it was kind of a competition between us, but usually my team would win," Selena joked to *Girls' Life Magazine*.

Selena has always enjoyed being one of the guys, so it's no surprise that one of her best friends growing up was a boy. His name is Randy Hill, Selena explained to *Girls' Life Magazine*. "Yeah, I knew him ever since I was five. He's really cool, and he's nice. People think, 'Oh yeah, she has a guy best friend.' Yeah, because I've known him my whole life. I know everything about him, and he's sweet. Yes, I have a guy and girl best friend." Selena made a lot of other good friends when school started as well, but most of them were boys, too. "I guess I'm a guys' girl. Back in Texas, where I'm from, I just hung out with my guy friends because they're all like older brothers. I got into a lot of drama with girls. They're very, 'Oh my gosh. She said this about you.' I was like, 'Whoa, OK. Too much drama.' Guys are like, 'Whatever,' and that's how I am," Selena told *Girls' Life Magazine*.

When Selena wasn't outside with her friends, she was usually making art, reading, or watching movies! Selena loved getting a chance to express herself creatively, as she explained to *Scholastic News*. "I like to draw and paint. I've been doing it ever since I could remember. I have no idea what I draw. I just draw anything that comes to mind. . . . I loved Dorothy and I loved the characters and I have the movie. I have no idea why, but I just loved that book [*The Wonderful Wizard of Oz*]."

Selena is still very close with her friends and family in Grand Prairie. Selena even takes two family keepsakes with her when she travels on location: "the promise ring that my dad gave to me when I was twelve and my grandmother's blanket," she told *Scholastic News*. Selena goes home to visit her family, too, as often as she possibly can. "My mom has always told me, 'Remember where you came from.' I was surrounded by the best people back home. I'll never forget that," Selena told *Discovery Girls*.

With the support of her friends and family, Selena

discovered a passion for performing that set her apart from the other kids her age. Mandy performed as a stage actress in nearby Dallas, Texas, and Selena loved watching her. It must have been very inspiring to see her mother's dedication to her dreams. Mandy never gave up on theater, even when times got tough. She taught Selena that hard work and dedication really do pay off, and that you always have to believe in yourself.

With so much talent in her family, it's really no surprise that Selena set her sights on performing when she was just a little girl. Mandy's continued success as a talented stage actress and makeup artist sparked Selena's interest in acting. "I watched my mom do a lot of theater when I was younger and I saw how much passion she had for it. I loved to watch her rehearse. I always wanted to get involved in that," Selena shared with *Scholastic News*. When Selena was about six years old, she decided that she, too, wanted to be an actress. Selena's mom knew better than to try to stop her determined daughter, so she took Selena to her first audition. "My mom did a lot of theater when I was younger so I grew up around it, and I just always loved it. I loved running lines with her, and then one day I tried out for something and got it, and it all started!" Selena told PBSKids.org. All that time Selena spent in theaters while her mother rehearsed or performed definitely paid off when it came time for her first audition.

Selena was a natural entertainer. She just seemed to know when to ham it up and when to tone it down. Selena always impressed casting agents with her comedic timing, but she was a little self-conscious about her looks. Most girls would love to have Selena's warm tan skin, expressive brown eyes, and wavy dark brown hair, but there was a time when Selena wished she looked different. "I wanted to be like my friends. I hung out with girls who had blue eyes and blond hair and I thought, 'I want to look like them!'" Selena explained to *TWIST* magazine. But Selena's more exotic look actually helped her when she began acting. And now she couldn't be more proud of her heritage. "When I went to auditions, I'd be in a room with a lot of blond girls, and I always stood out. It actually helped . . . that I looked different. It got me where I am today! I don't know if I would have had the opportunity to be on *Wizards of Waverly Place* if it weren't for my heritage. I realize everybody wants what they don't have. But at the end of the day, what you have inside is much more beautiful than what's on the outside!" Selena told *TWIST* magazine.

By the time Selena was seven years old, she knew she wanted to get involved in acting, but she never could have imagined what was in store for her. Her birthday that year would change Selena's life more than she could ever have expected. She would meet the girl who would go on to be her best friend for years to come, Demi Lovato, and get the chance to fulfill her dream of becoming an actress at the same time!

CHAPTER 2:
Bopping with Barney

Selena went to her very first audition in July, right around the time of her seventh birthday. "I got into it when I was six or seven. My mom did a lot of theater back in Dallas, Texas. I asked her if I could try acting, too. *Barney & Friends* was the first audition I went to and the first show I was ever on," Selena told *Time for Kids*.

The show Selena was auditioning for was the Public Broadcasting Service television series, *Barney & Friends*. The show has been a huge hit with both kids and parents since 1992. "I love you, you love me. We're a happy family . . ." sang Barney, the large purple plush dinosaur, to thousands of kids daily on PBS stations across the country. *Barney & Friends* is about Barney, Baby Bop, BJ, and Riff, a group of loveable and colorful plush dinosaurs. They sing, dance, tell stories, and play games with a cast of talented elementary school kids. The show has been a big success entertaining and teaching young children about manners, basic readiness skills, and personal safety.

Acting in the show was also one of the best opportunities for kids in Texas to break into show business. That's why on one hot July morning a long line of kids and their parents wound around the parking lot of The Studios at Las Colinas, in Irving, Texas. The children waiting in line were there for an open audition and a chance to be series regulars on *Barney & Friends*. Most of them had no acting experience, but they all wanted to be on the show they loved so much. The kids ranged in age from five to ten years old, were of different races, and had dramatically different looks. But they were all talented. Selena and her mom knew that the competition would be stiff, but they were willing to wait anyway, just for a shot at impressing the casting agents.

As Selena waited, she began to notice the little girl standing next to her. Her name was Demi Lovato, and she was six years old with long brown hair, bangs, round glasses, and a wide smile. The two girls smiled shyly at each other as they stood next to their mothers in line. They were both nervous and neither of them was very happy about the long wait. Selena told *Entertainment Weekly*, "It was scorching hot, July. We were in line with 1,400 kids and we happened to be standing right next to each other. She had a little bow in her hair, and she turned around and she looked at me and said, 'Do you want to color?' She laid her blue jean jacket down and we started to color." It was the storybook beginning of a fantastic friendship for Selena and Demi. They talked and giggled all morning about their families, school, and friends as the line slowly inched forward. Soon they were goofing around as if they'd been friends forever. By the time the girls made it to the front of the line, they didn't want to stop playing. They wished each other good luck and went in with their moms to the audition.

Selena was a little scared when it was her turn to audition. "I was definitely nervous; I was very shy when I was younger. . . . But then when I got to the audition, I realized it was just running lines, just like I always did with my mom. It was scary — and those situations are still scary for me — but it was fun at the same time," Selena told PBSKids.org. Even though she was nervous, Selena did a great job. She was called back to do a few more auditions, and then she got the call that she was on the show! She was so excited! Selena was cast as Gianna, and she was a hit from day one. She was funny and spunky, and a real asset to the show. In fact, Selena was often selected for funny scenes that required great comedic timing.

Of course, the best part of Selena's first day on set was discovering that her new friend from the audition line, Demi, was also cast on the show as Angela! Selena explained to *Entertainment Weekly*, "we had a couple of callbacks, and I saw her from the other side of the room and it was kind of a movie moment. We still joke about it." The two girls swapped numbers and immediately became good friends. They hung out together between takes on the set, after school, and on weekends.

Acting on the show was a wonderful experience for Selena, and she believes that starring on *Barney & Friends* helped her become the professional actress she is today. "I was about six or seven years old when I started with that," Selena told the *Fort Worth Star-Telegram*. "I actually learned a lot from that, because I didn't know anything. That was my first audition, my first anything I'd ever done. I think that was a real blessing." Working on *Barney* taught Selena many basic acting skills. She learned how to memorize and deliver lines, work with other actors, sing and dance on camera, and work with multiple cameras. Selena told *People*, "I was very shy when I was little," she recalls. "I didn't know what 'camera right' was. I didn't know what blocking was. I learned everything from *Barney*." Selena loved her work, and continued filming her role as Gianna on *Barney & Friends* for two seasons. She credits the show not only with giving her a start in show business, but also with helping her develop a real love for acting. "A lot of people would be embarrassed to say they were on *Barney* but I embrace the fact and I had such a wonderful time doing that show," Selena explained to Maggie Rodriguez on *The Early Show*.

Even though Selena's life as an actress was very cool, it wasn't always easy. Not everyone at Selena's school was supportive. In fact, some of Selena's so-called friends were very jealous of her success. "I'd miss a couple of weeks for *Barney* and then I'd go back to school and

I'd deal with some jealousy. I wouldn't talk about the show unless somebody said, 'How was your episode?' So not a lot of people were jealous — just this one group of girls who didn't like me," Selena told *Discovery Girls*. It was hard for Selena to deal with her friends turning on her like that. The girls were popular and they tried to make Selena look bad in front of all of their classmates. "Popularity isn't what you think it is," Selena tells *J-14* magazine. "It's much better to be yourself rather than trying to be cool. Popularity never leads to anything good." The mean girls in Selena's school spread awful rumors about her, and Selena was faced with having to "live down a bad reputation." Rather than give in to the spiteful girls, Selena decided that they just weren't worth it. "You can't get involved, fire back or do anything," Selena continued to *J-14* magazine. "If people say, 'I heard you did this,' just say, 'I'm sorry, that's not true!' At the end of the day, I really ended up finding out who my true friends were."

Luckily Selena had enough self-confidence to rise above the drama. She separated herself from them as much as she could and focused on her own things — and it definitely paid off in the long run! She hung out with her real friends and continued to focus on her career. "I mean, I got made fun of because I was in *Barney*! Just know that, at the end of the day, you will be okay and you'll always have your true friends with you." Selena said to *Discovery Girls*, "They've even come out to Los Angeles to see the show. . . . I did lose a couple of friends because of the whole jealousy thing. But I look at it like a sport. Some kids play soccer. Acting is my sport."

Selena filmed episodes of *Barney & Friends* through the end of fifth grade. She and Demi Lovato spent a lot of time together on and off the show, and became true best friends during that time. Soon the girls became nearly inseparable, getting together to play and having sleep-overs at each other's houses. They didn't go to the same school but lived close enough to get together often. Best of all, Selena and Demi had each other to rely on. Other kids at school may not have understood why acting was so important to Selena, but Demi always understood perfectly! "My favorite thing [about Demi] is that she is very honest," says Selena. "She doesn't hide anything, so when we have problems, she comes to me immediately and wants to clear it up. She's like a sister to me, and it's awesome. It's insane how many things we have been through together. We've seen each other through first boyfriends and first girl drama and things like that," Selena explained to *Girls' Life Magazine*. They helped each other through fights with other friends, boy trouble, and the disappointments of bad auditions. They also celebrated together when they made good grades, met cute boys, aced auditions, and landed amazing roles.

Selena and Demi worked on their careers together, too. They took some of the same acting classes and would often ride to auditions together. They never let going after the same roles get in the way of their friendship, which was very important to both girls. Selena told *Entertainment Weekly*, "We were inseparable after doing two seasons together, and our moms are best friends now. Later, we homeschooled together, went on auditions together, everything." When Selena and Demi first met, they had no idea how successful they would be in the future, and they certainly never imagined that they would be big Disney stars just a few years later.

Barney & Friends was an amazing opportunity for Selena, and she wouldn't trade her time on the show for anything. The show taught her all about working in the industry and it was a great way to start her career. Plus, she met her best friend Demi Lovato through the show, and she is so glad to have such an incredible friendship in her life. "But we've both been working since we were six to get where we are, and we're just there to be proud of each other. We both know we're really, really lucky girls," Selena admitted to *Entertainment Weekly*. Plus there are very few people who can actually say that they got their show business start singing along with a large purple dinosaur named Barney!

CHAPTER 3:
The Road to Fame

After filming *Barney & Friends*, Selena knew that she wanted to be a professional actress. She loved her work on *Barney* and was excited to take on different and challenging roles. To prepare for auditions, Selena took classes with Demi from Cathryn Sullivan at EveryBody Fits studio in Coppell, Texas. EveryBody Fits studio had classes in everything from acting, music, and theater to gymnastics, tae kwon do, and dance. Cathryn, an excellent teacher, was also the mother of a child actor herself so she knew what she was talking about. Cody Linley has appeared many times in the role of Jake Ryan on episodes of the hit Disney Channel show *Hannah*

Montana, and starred in several made-for-television movies. Cody became friends with Selena and Demi when they took acting and singing classes together. With Cathryn's help and encouragement, Selena's singing, acting, and dancing skills improved even more, and she began auditioning for new roles.

Selena started out with auditions in Texas. With its generally pleasant weather and varied landscapes, Texas is a great place to shoot commercials, movies, and television shows. That was good news for Selena since it meant there were always auditions for her to go on. She landed parts in a number of commercials, and filmed national spots for Wal-Mart, Hasbro, and T.G.I. Fridays. Then, when Selena was eleven years old, she landed her first cameo role in a major movie. It was a very small part as the "water park girl" in 2003's *Spy Kids 3-D: Game Over*, the third installment in Robert Rodriguez's *Spy Kids* movie franchise. The *Spy Kids* trilogy is about the son and daughter of spies. The kids get the chance to save the world when their parents get into trouble. In *Spy Kids 3-D*, the daughter gets sucked into an evil video game and her brother has to save her. Selena played the girl at the water park. Even though Selena's part was very small, it was a role in a feature film and she learned a lot and was so proud. Plus, going to the movies with friends to see herself in 3-D was totally cool! And the rest of the cast was incredible. Selena got to work with big name stars like Alexa Vega, Daryl Sabara, Sylvester Stallone, Antonio Banderas, and Salma Hayek. Selena was really excited to be a part of a film with so many incredible stars of Hispanic heritage. She was especially inspired by Latino actress Salma, who encouraged Selena to be proud of her own Mexican heritage.

After *Spy Kids 3-D: Game Over*, Selena's next role was on a made-for-television movie of the popular show *Walker, Texas Ranger*. *Walker* has very devoted fans who love the show and its star, Chuck Norris, who plays the lead character in the series. The film first aired on

October 16, 2005. It was called *Walker, Texas Ranger: Trial by Fire,* and Selena played the part of Julie Walker. The show is about Cordell Walker, a Texas Ranger who takes the law into his own hands when dealing with criminals. The movie was a hit with *Walker* fans, and Selena enjoyed being a part of such a successful and long running show about Texas. It was extra cool for her since she had watched with her grandmother while she was growing up!

The next project that Selena landed was a pilot for a new children's show called *Brain Zapped.* It was written, directed, and produced by a local filmmaker named Eliud George Garcia. Selena was cast in the lead role of Emily Grace Garcia and she recorded the show's theme song. The show was about reading, and the adventures that can be found inside books. In the pilot, Selena's character, Emily, and her best friend Kingston, played by Lewis Parry, hear about something strange going on at their library. Both kids love books, so they decide to investigate.

Things seem normal when they arrive, but then they see holograms popping out of books and mysterious glowing bookshelves. Soon, the two friends are sucked into one of the bookshelves and are off on a series of adventures.

Most of the episode was shot on a green screen with just Selena and Lewis. Working in front of a green screen was a cool new experience for Selena. It meant that she and her co-star did all their acting while standing in a special all-green room. Then, during the editing process, the editor replaces all the green with any pre-shot background for the scene. The green screen made it easy for the director to add special effects and to make it *seem* like Selena had to journey back to prehistoric times with dinosaurs or to the North Pole. But in reality, Selena never had to leave Texas at all!

Brain Zapped made a decent showing at film festivals in 2006, but it was never picked up by a network, which was a little disappointing for Selena. She has always loved reading and she thought the show had a great message. Luckily for Selena's fans, the pilot is available on DVD for anyone who wants to see it!

But before Selena did *Brian Zapped*, she began to feel that she may have outgrown all of the acting opportunities in Texas, but she wasn't ready to give up on her dreams. She was really hoping to work on another television series. Selena loved working on *Barney & Friends*, but for her next project she was hoping to get a starring role. So when she heard about an open casting call in Dallas for the Disney Channel, she begged her mother to let her go. In fact, Selena and her BFF, Demi, both decided to go. Little did Selena know that that audition would eventually make her a superstar!

CHAPTER 4:
Disney Dreams

In the summer of 2004, one of the biggest names in the entertainment business, the Disney Channel, began a worldwide casting search for promising young talent. Selena and Demi attended the local audition in nearby Dallas, Texas, with their moms. Selena was only twelve years old, but she knew it was the chance of a lifetime! Selena must have been very nervous, knowing that she would be competing against thousands of other talented girls, but she was ready for the challenge. She had her mom and best friend there for support, and, after all, Selena's two years on *Barney & Friends* had given her both the experience and the confidence that she needed to take advantage of such a fantastic opportunity.

The audition was a success! Selena totally delighted the casting agents with her talent and spunky attitude. They were so impressed that three weeks later they asked Selena to audition again with a very select group of candidates for the head honchos at Disney. "They flew us out to California. It was definitely scary. I was in this room full of executives and I was testing against girls who have done movies," Selena explained to *Variety*. Even though Selena was facing some pretty intense competition, she aced the audition. Her talent, professionalism, and ability to deliver an inspiring performance when the pressure was on made Selena stand out from the crowd.

One of the executives supervising Selena's audition was Gary Marsh, the president of entertainment for Disney Channels Worldwide. Gary told *Entertainment Weekly*

that Selena's audition was "green, it was rough — but she had that It Factor." Since Gary was in charge of casting and developing new series for the Disney Channel, he was an expert at recognizing rising talent when he saw it. "We don't look at television as the endgame," he explained to *Entertainment Weekly*. "That's the launch pad. . . . We go into this thinking we are going to build a star; it's not thinking we are casting a role." Gary and the rest of the Disney executives definitely wanted Selena Gomez to become part of the Disney family. She had the talent and the image they wanted, and they were counting on her to sing, dance, and act her way to Disney stardom. Selena and her family were thrilled by the news.

First, Disney asked Selena to film the pilot for *What's Stevie Thinking?* — a spin-off of the hit Disney series *Lizzie McGuire*. The pilot starred Selena and veteran Disney actress Lalaine Vergara-Paras, who played Miranda Sanchez, Lizzie's best friend on the *Lizzie McGuire* show.

The pilot *What's Stevie Thinking?*, followed Miranda as she started at a new high school away from her old *Lizzie* friends. She shared her trials and experiences with Stevie, her younger sister, who was played by Selena. Much of the show revolved around the relationship between the two sisters and their family. Selena was very excited to be offered the role because she'd always been a big fan of *Lizzie McGuire*. But, even more exciting to Selena, *What's Stevie Thinking?* was slated to be the first Disney Channel series to star a Latino family.

Selena had always been a little disappointed that few television shows featured girls that looked like her, or even had families that celebrated the same traditions and holidays that her family did. Having an opportunity to showcase her culture in a popular television show was very attractive to Selena. She had so much fun shooting the pilot and working with the cast and crew. They were all very proud of *What's Stevie Thinking?*, but unfortunately test audiences weren't as interested in the show as the Disney Channel had hoped they would be. Disney decided not to pick up the series. Selena was disappointed, but felt confident that her chance would come.

Even though *What's Stevie Thinking?* didn't make it into production, filming the pilot had generated a lot of exposure for Selena in Hollywood. Soon, Disney's biggest competitor, Nickelodeon, contacted Selena. Selena and her agent met several times with their development executives and she even auditioned for a Nickelodeon pilot and a made-for-television movie. But somehow Nickelodeon just didn't click for Selena. "It was uncomfortable," she explained to *Entertainment Weekly*, "like I was cheating on Disney." Selena felt completely comfortable and at home with the Disney Channel, and really wanted to work there. It was obvious that Disney wanted to keep Selena, too! They quickly developed two new pilots, offering choice roles to Selena. "That's a question of betting on talent," Gary Marsh explained to *Variety*.

"Once you find the person, you've got to make a commitment to give them work to get their shot." Disney was committed to making Selena a star, and they felt sure that they would produce one of the new pilots. "Disney was like, 'Let's put you in everything we have,'" Selena's mother, Mandy, happily told *Entertainment Weekly*.

A spin-off from *The Suite Life of Zack & Cody* was the first new pilot. The show starred Arwin, the maintenance man from the Tipton Hotel. In the show, he moves in with his sister to help her look after her kids. Selena was cast as one of Arwin's nieces, Alexa. Ultimately, the show didn't test well with audiences and Disney decided to move on to the next pilot for Selena instead.

The second pilot, called *Wizards of Waverly Place*, was a fresh comedy about a family of wizards living in New York City. The three siblings, Justin, Alex, and Max, were secretly learning to use their magic, while going to school and helping their parents run a sandwich shop. The show was a unique mix of comedy and special effects that was perfect for Selena. Selena's character was Alex, the only girl in the family, and the most mischievous and challenging character on the show. Selena loved filming the pilot; she thought the show was very good, and she felt completely in sync with the rest of the cast. When the filming was completed, Selena and her mom went home to Texas and waited to find out if the show would be picked up. Luckily, she didn't have long to wait. The test audiences absolutely loved it! Disney decided to make a few changes, but Selena wasn't one of them. They signed her up for the first season and then locked the rest of the cast in place. Selena was actually very excited about the changes. The original script had been about a family with Irish heritage and had been called "The Amazing Hannigans" and then "The Amazing O'Malleys." There had also been more kids in the original show. But Disney decided to cut down the cast to three children and changed the family's last name to Russo. Instead of being Irish, they would be Mexican and Italian. Selena loved that change, since she had always wanted to work on a show about a Hispanic family.

Selena was more than ready to start filming *Wizards of Waverly Place* as soon as she got the news it had been green-lit. The only downside was that Selena and her family would have to move to Los Angeles. "The biggest challenge was moving away from home, and at first, I didn't know how I was gonna do it. Once I came out to L. A. and started working, I adjusted a little bit but I'm still a Texas girl. My escape is to go home and relax for a bit, which I get to do when we're on hiatuses," Selena explained to *Popstar!* It was difficult for Selena to leave her friends and family and make the big move. It didn't help that money had always been a little tight for Selena's mom and stepfather, and moving to California was going to be expensive! Luckily, Disney was willing to pay for the move in order to give Selena her chance for success. They really believed in her! "Without Disney, we wouldn't be out here at all," Selena's mom, Mandy, explained to *Entertainment Weekly.* "We're a paycheck-to-paycheck family, and they kept paying for everything."

Since Disney needed Selena in Hollywood as soon as possible, she and her mom moved to Los Angeles right away. Selena's mom was able to bring her production company along with her to Los Angeles, and Selena's stepfather stayed behind temporarily to take care of their home and four dogs before joining his family in California. It was a big challenge for the whole family to move. Everything was in Texas — jobs, friends, family, school, and their home. But it was the right choice. Selena knew she was very lucky to have such a supportive mom and step-dad that were willing to help her achieve her dreams, no matter what it took! "It was sad to say good-bye to my friends and family, but it was a happy moment, too. They were so proud of me for achieving my dreams," Selena told *Discovery Girls.*

Since Disney helped Selena and her mom with everything, they began to feel at home in Los Angeles right away. They rented a hip, loft apartment in a renovated building in downtown Los Angeles. Even though she missed her house in Texas, the new apartment was the perfect home for the hottest new Disney star! Selena must have been really excited to begin decorating her new room, although it probably had to wait for awhile. As soon as she moved in, Disney was ready to put Selena to work. They booked her in guest appearances and promotional spots so that Disney fans could get to know Selena before her show aired.

Selena was a guest star on two of Disney's most popular shows at the time, *Hannah Montana* and *The Suite Life of Zack & Cody*. Selena's first guest role was on *The Suite Life of Zack & Cody* in an episode called "A Midsummer's Nightmare." Selena played Gwen, the character who was dating Cody. During the episode, all the kids tried out for a production of *A Midsummer*

Night's Dream. When Selena's character had to kiss Zack's character in the play, crazy things began to happen! Gwen liked kissing Zack so much that she dumped Cody. Then the brothers got into a huge, very goofy fight onstage during the play. It was a fun episode to film, and it was also a big first for Selena as an actress — she got to give her first on-screen kiss! "My first [on-screen kiss] was with Dylan Sprouse on *The Suite Life of Zack & Cody.* That was fun. He was shorter than me, so I had to bend down a little bit, but it was a cute episode," Selena told *Girls' Life Magazine*. Selena handled it really well, even though she was probably pretty nervous about kissing such a hot guy in front of all the cast and crew! Even though there is no real romantic interest between Selena and either of the Sprouse twins, Cole and Dylan, Selena has a close friendship that started with her very first guest appearance!

Next, Selena was invited to guest star on *Hannah Montana*. She played Hannah's biggest rival, Mikayla, who was an up-and-coming pop diva bent on stealing all of Hannah's fans. Selena had a blast playing mean girl Mikayla. Her character was really nice when cameras were filming or fans were around, but she changed into a competitive, bratty diva when she was alone with Hannah. Selena got to do some crazy scenes and wear some fun stylish clothes and makeup as part of her role. Fans loved her so much that Selena was asked to appear as Mikayla on several more episodes. It was really a fun part to play, battling Hannah for awards, fans, and cute guys!

Selena and Miley Cyrus, the show's star, who plays both Miley Stewart and Hannah Montana, became good friends during filming. The two girls really enjoyed hanging out together on the set, and talking about music, clothes, and boys. Of course, being friends with Miley just made it harder for Selena to be mean to her when the cameras were rolling. "Me and Miley [Cyrus of *Hannah Montana*] would do a scene where we're mad and saying mean things, and when they'd cut, we would run up to each other and say 'I'm so sorry.' People would laugh and they're like, 'You're just acting,' and we're like, 'I know, but I feel so bad,'" Selena explained to *Girls' Life Magazine*. Tabloids have tried to spread rumors that Selena and Miley are rivals in real life, too, but they are actually still good friends to this day. Selena told *OK!* magazine that, "We call all of that 'Disney High' because it's basically like being in high school, but times a thousand. You know you have to handle it as you would in a normal school and I do that by surrounding myself with positive things and people who really care about me. We just laugh about it." The girls continue to be friends, and since they are both part of the Disney family, they still see each other all the time at Disney events, premieres, and parties. They may even work together again someday!

With several popular guest spots to her credit, Selena was more than ready to begin filming her own show. Once she walked onto the set of the *Wizards of Waverly*

Place and the camera started rolling, she blew everyone away with her spunk, talent, and comedic timing. The Disney Channel knew right away that they had a hit on their hands. Selena Gomez had finally made it — and Disney would never be the same!

CHAPTER 5:
Wizards of Waverly Place

In 2007, Selena's dream to star in a Disney Channel Original Series finally came true. After months of waiting and several failed pilots, Selena was cast in the lead role of Alex Russo in *Wizards of Waverly Place*. Selena was incredibly excited, especially since she got to play the only girl in a magical family living in New York City.

Wizards of Waverly Place is all about the Russo family. The Russos own and run a neighborhood sandwich shop on Waverly Place called the Waverly Sub Station. To the public the Russos seem like the average New York family, but they actually have a very big secret — each of the three Russo kids has magical powers! Justin, sixteen, played by David Henrie; Alex, fourteen, played by Selena; and Max, twelve, played by Jake T. Austin, have inherited magical powers from their dad, Jerry. Unfortunately only one child from each wizarding family is allowed to keep his or her magical powers as an adult. After they come of age, a family competition will determine who gets to keep their wizard status. Until then, all three kids must learn as much as they can about using their magic, while also learning to function in the regular world. "The kids are learning magic from their father. But at the same time, we still go to school and deal with issues that any other normal teenager would. Our friends and classmates don't know that we can do magic, so we lead kind of a double life," Selena explained to *Time for Kids*. Of course, having magical powers sounds really cool, but they also get the Russos into a lot of very funny situations. "They will definitely get a lot of laughs. The parents are going to get a lot out of this, too. It's such a family-based show," Selena told *Time for Kids*.

Family is a big part of *Wizards*, since the whole Russo family definitely has to work together to keep their magic a secret from the rest of the world. When Dad, Jerry Russo, played by David DeLuise, isn't running the sandwich shop, he is holding daily wizard training classes in their home's secret "lair." Jerry lost his own magical abilities when his brother became the family wizard, but he is a great teacher. Alex and Max aren't always the best students, but Jerry does his best to teach his kids the proper way to perform spells and use magical objects. His most difficult challenge is helping clean up his kids' magical messes when they don't follow his rules!

Of course, Jerry does have help from his wife, Theresa Russo, played by Maria Canals Barrera. While helping to run the sandwich shop, she teaches her children the importance of their Latino heritage, offers motherly advice, and tries to stay one step ahead of her children's mishaps, magical or otherwise. "It is a lot of fun to be the Disney mom, [it] is what I feel like I am. Especially because the parts have been so well written, so beautifully written, the parents have been so integral to the story. . . . I love playing Theresa!" Maria told *TV Guide*. Theresa is Mexican and Jerry's family is Italian, so they try to integrate traditions from both sides of the family into their kids' lives.

Justin is the oldest Russo child. He is disciplined, studious, and a total overachiever. He desperately wants to be cool, and his siblings tease him a lot for being a nerd. But when Alex and Max get into trouble, Justin is always there to help them out of it. "He [Justin] tends to do what is right, and he keeps everyone in check," David Henrie told *TV Guide*. Justin and Alex have a very close relationship. Unlike her big brother, Alex is not disciplined, studious, or much of an overachiever. Instead, Alex loves to have a good time and will go out of her way to avoid hard work, but she has a good heart and always does the right thing in the end. "Alex is the only girl of the three kids, so she has their dad wrapped around her finger.

Also, because she's been raised with boys her entire life, she's got a little tomboyish twist. Alex is the sibling who gets into the most trouble," Selena explained to *Time for Kids*. Alex is spunky and popular, and never hesitates to use her magic to take the easy way out. In fact, "cast magic first, ask questions later is her motto," according to Disney.com. Max, the youngest, has just come into his powers, so he is not quite as far along in his magical training as Justin and Alex. But what Max lacks in magic, he makes up for in comedy! Max isn't particularly smart and his wacky, zany, and somewhat dim-witted ideas are always hilarious. Max and Alex get along very well on the show and often team up to pull a prank on Justin.

Of course, it isn't all in the family! Alex's best friend is Harper, played by Jennifer Stone. Harper is a wannabe fashionista who loves wearing wacky-themed outfits — like a dress covered in rubber duckies or an entire outfit made of waxed fruit! Harper doesn't know about the family's magical abilities during the first season, but she does spend a lot of time with the Russo family. Since Alex is always in trouble, Harper is often her partner in crime. But Harper also spends a lot of time trying to get Justin to notice her since she has a huge crush on him! In season two, Harper finally learns the truth about the Russo family's magic. "It's kinda nice to have just Jennifer as the person to come into our lair, and in on different sets she's never been able to go to, so it's kinda nice to include her more," Selena told *TV Guide*.

Selena loves playing Alex, but it hasn't always been easy to get into character. Selena is sweet, hardworking, and very responsible, so playing sassy troublemaker Alex has been a challenge! The two may be different, but they do share a similar sense of style as Selena explained to *Time for Kids*, "I don't get into as much trouble as Alex does, but I do like the Converse sneakers she wears. Alex has kind of a funky, laid-back, individual style. I think that's something we share." Luckily, the writers and producers of the show really let Selena give Alex her own twists. "I asked that they keep her edgy. I don't want to be wearing heels. She wears Converse, and she's cool. I'm not really a girly girl," Selena mentioned in a chat with *Entertainment Weekly* at the start of season one. Alex has become more and more of a troublemaker as the series has progressed, but that's okay with Selena. As she explained to *Teen* magazine, that's one of Selena's favorite parts about playing Alex, "she's always getting into trouble and she's doing stuff that I wish I could do. At the end of the day it's all fake! I don't want to get in trouble and make a mess, but it's nice to pretend that it was real!"

Disney Channel executives were certainly right to believe that the show would be a success! After the premiere of *Wizards of Waverly Place* on October 12, 2007, they were thrilled as the popularity of the show grew with each episode that aired. Disney quickly got the writers working on a second season, and Selena and the rest of the cast are hoping for a third. The writers even conjured up a special one hour summer school episode that aired in April 2008! In the special, Justin and Alex go to summer school at Wiz Tech, a spoof on *Harry Potter*'s Hogwarts School of Witchcraft and Wizardry. Fans loved the funny, good-humored satire, and the show had a record number of viewers!

With each season Selena has had the chance to develop her character more and more. She's absolutely loved working as Alex and watching her grow from episode to episode. "I think she goes through situations with her family and her friendships and she kinda has this huge relationship drama and you kinda see just a more mature side to her, which is nice." Selena explained to *TV Guide*. And, of course, as Alex grows up she goes through a lot of situations that fans can totally relate to — like fighting with friends, getting her license, and dating boys! "She gets her first boyfriend," Selena told MTV News. His name is Dean, "and he's just this really sweet guy who, I honestly think, has a lot of potential.

I think he's going to do great." She added that he doesn't know the family secret yet!

Fans definitely love the show, and they proved it at the 2009 Kids' Choice Awards. Selena was super thrilled to win the 2009 Award for Favorite TV Actress for her role as Alex in *Wizards of Waverly Place*. Selena knows that this fan award is the most important nomination of the year and she was so happy that her fans thought so much of her and the show!

So what's up next for the Russos? A Disney Channel Original Movie of *Wizards of Waverly Place*! Selena and the rest of the cast were psyched when they found out they would get to film a whole movie, especially since they knew the writers would come up with something extra special for their fans. Everyone's lips have been sealed about the plot, but Selena did tell MTV News that, "I think it would have to be that our secret is about to be exposed!" Fans will absolutely love the movie according-ing to co-star David Henrie. He explained to MTV News what fans can expect. "Lots of crazy cool stuff — big wizard battles. We are going to be in the tropical forest, so [there's] lots of adventure. The premise is we win a trip and go on vacation." The movie was filmed in Puerto Rico, which was extra cool for the Los Angeles–based cast. They loved getting to hang out in the tropical paradise. Keep an eye out for the premiere of this super special *Wizards of Waverly Place* event. It's sure to have lots of twists and surprises — including cameos from other Disney stars!

CHAPTER 6:
Behind the Scenes Magic

Wizards of Waverly Place is an incredibly cool show, but filming it every week is even cooler! Selena and her Wizards of Waverly Place family have learned a lot about working with unusual sets and magical, special effects props. "It's really cool. We've been up in harnesses. We've worked with animals and voiceovers . . . The special effects add a different level to the Disney Channel," Selena told Time for Kids. In fact, the cast has done some pretty crazy things while filming Wizards of Waverly Place. "Oh, man! Where do I begin? I've had to pour chocolate all over myself. I've had mashed potatoes in my hair. We've 'flown' magic carpets. I get turned into [a] tiger in one episode! I think this show's all about the craziness, and we've done a lot of crazy stuff here," Selena explained to *Time for Kids*.

"The show is definitely something different from other Disney Channel shows," Selena told *Time for Kids*. Whether it's learning to drive a magic carpet or conjuring up a pocket elf to help with a Spanish test, the Russo kids learn the good, the bad, and the often very funny consequences of using their magic. When asked by *Teen* magazine if she believed in magic, Selena said, "I think a little bit, I kind of do. I think it's cool to sort of step into something supernatural." Before taking on the role of Alex, Selena had never been much of a fan of fantasy. She didn't watch the *Harry Potter* movies or read the books, so she had to do her homework on all things wizard-related fast! Selena explained to *Teen* magazine, "Our show's not as dark. It's lighter and it's a sitcom, so it's funny. We try to get in trouble, and, of course, with magic it's easy to get into trouble."

"Everywhere there's Alex, there's drama," Selena commented to *TV Guide* about her character, Alex Russo. In some of Selena's favorite episodes, Alex finds herself in very big trouble! As she told PBSKids.org, "The quinceañera episode was probably my favorite, or the episode where Alex wanted to go to a rated R movie. She tries to put a spell on herself to magically go into the movie theater, but she ends up actually IN the movie, so she's stuck in this scary movie sorority-house flick, and they shot it just like a movie. It was so much fun because it was like being able to shoot an actual scary movie." Getting to be the troublemaker is always fun for Selena. She'd never break the rules or talk back to her parents in real life, but getting to do it on the show is pretty cool. That way she gets to have the fun — but she never gets grounded for real!

Magic is such a fun part of the *Wizards of Waverly Place* shows. What kind of spell would Selena perform if she were a wizard? She told *Time for Kids*, "I've always wanted to be able to zap food to anywhere at any time. For example, if you're sitting on the couch craving pizza, you could say a spell, and boom! It's right there." What other magic from the show does she wish she could do in real life? "Clone myself! Just to get out of class, it would be nice!" Selena says laughingly to *Teen* magazine.

Kids easily relate to the Russo siblings on *Wizards of Waverly Place*, even though they don't have magic themselves, because the characters are so realistic. After all, the show is really about family and everyone can relate to that. Selena told PBSKids.org, "My favorite scenes are ones where all of the family is together. Whether it's a funny or dramatic scene, whether we're trying to solve a problem or doing magic or turning my brother invisible, it comes off best when we're with the whole family in the loft. I think when we're all together the show is at its strongest point. And I love being with the entire cast in a scene." Episodes cover issues that everyone can relate to: sports, fashion, drama, school work, jobs, school, grades, crushes, dating, dances, friends, and family. "There are always times when you wish you could be invisible when something embarrassing happens. Or you wish you could rewind time because you just tripped in front of everybody. That's why I think kids will like the show. We bring to life everything that they imagine and dream about," Selena explained to *Time for Kids.*

Of course, it's not all fun on the set. Selena, Jen, and Jake all spend the legally required limit of five hours a school day with a tutor on-set and their shooting schedule allows plenty of time for study! They have to finish their homework before they can do anything else. But when the stars aren't filming a scene or sitting in class, they can relax and hang out. Everyone on the cast enjoys sitting around and talking between shoots, Selena explained to *Girls' Life Magazine.* "Well, David has these cards with questions like, 'Would you treat your kids the way your parents treat you?' They're conversation cards, and you can ask each other what's your embarrassing moment and stuff. Other than that, we talk and laugh. If we're tired, we all just lounge together. David likes to hit the back of my knee so I almost trip. He's always doing that. We just get silly and play patty-cake or something." Selena texts and e-mails her friends from her trailer, gossips with Jen, and shoots hoops with Jake. "We actually have [a basketball court] on set. It's fun," Selena told *Girls' Life Magazine*. "I only take on [my TV brother], so when I beat him it's not a good feeling. He's only twelve and half the time he beats me."

Jake also taught Selena how to surf this year, as she explained to PBSKids.org, "Yes, Jake recently did a movie where he surfed, and he told me I should try it. And I was like, 'Okay,' and I got really into it, it was so much fun. At first the ocean scared me a little bit, but we don't go too far out. Once you ride that first wave, there's something about it that keeps you riding more and more! . . . It's a stress relief. . . . It's nice to go on a beach and just forget about stuff and get away. It's fun. And acting's kind of like a sport for me, too, it's the same as something like football or basketball for other people. It's something you do for fun and something you're serious about." Now Selena is totally hooked and surfs as much as she can.

The cast of *Wizards of Waverly Place* has become very close during the filming of the series. Selena told *Teen* magazine, "It's been so much fun just to develop a new family and to have new friends. They're my second family, and everyone on there is so nice and so sweet. They're my real brothers and second parents!" Selena loves her television brothers, David and Jake, and considers them to be two of her best friends. Hanging out with them on the set all day is really fun for her. "I can't even explain it! I am very confident when I say that we are the closest cast that the Disney Channel has ever had. We've been told that because we spend every waking moment with each other — it's insane! Jake [Austin], Jen [Stone],

David [Henrie], and I do karaoke together, we go to the movies, and we go surfing every weekend. And as soon as we get off work, we text and call each other. My mom is always like, 'You act like you never see each other!' We've just gotten so close," Selena told *Discovery Girls*.

Spending so much time with David and Jake has been good for Selena. "I'm the only child, so it's really cool to play the middle sister of two brothers on *Wizards*. It's cool to pretend I've known these people all my life and get in fights with them. It's really fun," Selena tells *Girls' Life Magazine*. It's the first time she has experienced what it would be like to have brothers, and she loves it! She further explains to PBSKids.org, "they basically ARE my brothers; they're my real family. My mom laughs at me all the time because we're constantly in touch with one another off the set, we're always calling. They're always there for me, and it's torture when I can't see them every day. We do fight like brothers and sisters sometimes, but mostly we play around and joke around. I don't have any real life siblings so this way I can have brothers." Selena even admitted to *Girls' Life Magazine*, "I cried when the first season was over because my little brother [Jake T. Austin] was going back to New York, and my older brother [David Henrie] was going to Utah to shoot *Dadnapped*. So we call each other every day, 'What are you doing? I miss you.'" What is the most surprising part about having brothers? Selena tells PBSKids.org, "They're both so protective of me. Even when I like a boy or something, they have to make sure he's okay, or the boy has to be 'approved' by them." Selena and Jennifer are good friends in real life, too. "Actually we [Selena and Jennifer] don't fight as much as Alex and Harper do. They have fights almost every episode — that's only because it's a part of growing up, but for us, we're just kinda chill. I think we're the opposite of Alex and Harper!" Selena tells *TV Guide*.

Before the first episode of *Wizards of Waverly Place* even aired, Selena and the rest of the cast quickly made fans out of everyone who came to watch their tapings. Fans loved the crazy magic and the warm family dynamic. But it was Alex who really won their hearts! Selena enjoys performing the live tapings in front of an audience. It must be so exciting when the audience laughs at the funny elements the cast has been rehearsing all week! Selena has been so grateful for her fans who come to watch the tapings. She told *Discovery Girls*, "It was actually a surprise because I didn't think I'd have fans until the show came out. But Jake and I have been stopped before. They'll say, 'We went to one of your tapings!' It's such a cool feeling when fans come up to you because they're so excited and nervous. Meanwhile, I'm thinking, 'I'm more excited and nervous than you are right now!' It's pretty cool."

Selena was very proud of *Wizards of Waverly Place* and she was thrilled that fans loved the show as much as she did. It's now one of Disney's most popular shows, which is hard for Selena to believe sometimes. She's a long way since that first Disney audition! Selena has worked so hard to be successful, and she is happy to think she can be a good role model for her fans, especially other Latino girls. "It's the coolest feeling in the world to be able to make a kid's day by smiling at them," says Selena to *People*.

CHAPTER 7:
Big Screen Queen

Filming *Wizards of Waverly Place* every week has been a dream come true for Selena. She really enjoys developing her character, Alex, and working with all her friends on the Disney Studios set. But working on the show every week isn't always as challenging as Selena would like. Selena wants to be an actress with a long career filled with diverse roles. She knows it's important for her career that she try her hand at something new once in a while. Luckily, *Wizards of Waverly Place* doesn't film year-round. Selena has several months off at a time, and instead of taking it easy, energetic Selena uses the time to ...on for new roles and film movies.

Filming a movie is different than filming a television show — the sets are bigger, the cameras are different, and you work with one script for months instead of getting a new script every week. But what really drew Selena to movies was that it's interesting and challenging to work with new people on location. Filming movies is very appealing to Selena, since they give her a chance to play different types of characters and extend her range as an actress.

Selena is very particular about the types of roles she takes on. She doesn't say yes to just anything. She only accepts roles that she thinks will broaden her acting skills and appeal to her current fans. Selena reads every script her agent sends her very carefully and always talks them over with her parents. She is very careful not to choose any roles that require her to do anything she isn't completely comfortable with. She also stays away from roles that she feels won't be challenging enough or roles that will limit her ability to book other roles in the future. Selena actually turned down a starring role in

High School Musical 3: Senior Year, the first feature film in the Disney *High School Musical* franchise, for just that reason. *High School Musical* is possibly the most successful made-for-television movie of all time. It catapulted its stars, Zac Efron, Vanessa Hudgens, Ashley Tisdale, and Corbin Bleu, to superstardom. "*High School Musical 3* is cute, and I think it would be a great opportunity for someone else," Selena explained to the *New York Daily News*. "But I passed on it because I didn't want to do it. I plan to take other roles in acting that are challenging for me." Lots of other actresses would have loved to have been offered that part, but Selena didn't want to be looked at as just a Disney actress. She wanted to make sure people knew she could work outside of Disney as well. *High School Musical* fans were disappointed that Selena didn't join the cast, but Selena couldn't take a role just because the movie was sure to be a big hit. She has to take roles because they appeal to her, and it's really ʼful that Selena trusts her own judgment so much.

It shows just how much confidence Selena has in herself and her abilities.

One role that really did appeal to Selena was providing the voice for Helga in the animated smash hit, *Horton Hears a Who!*, based on the classic Dr. Seuss story. "I had never done animation, so I thought it would be cool to try something different, Selena told the *New York Daily News*. "I remember reading his books like crazy with my grandmother when I was younger," she added. Selena had long been a Dr. Seuss fan and she loved the story. *Horton Hears a Who!* is the story of an elephant named Horton who discovers an entire world of creatures called Whos existing on a daisy. Horton befriends one of the Whos, and decides it's up to him to keep them safe. Horton then must face some dangerous and often silly situations before he gets the Whos and their world to a safe place. The film builds upon the original book, expanding the characters and their world, and breathes new life into the familiar story.

Getting the opportunity to bring one of her favorite childhood books to life would be cool for anyone, but what made the film even cooler were Selena's amazing co-stars. The two largest roles in the film were played by famous comedians: Horton was played by Jim Carrey and The Mayor of Whoville was played by Steve Carell. Selena played Steve Carell's daughters in the film — all ninety of them! They were all named Helga and since they each had a different look and personality, Selena had to come up with a voice for each. "I voiced all of them," Selena explained to the *New York Daily News*. "I had to change up my voice to do higher voices, and then bring it down to do lower voices. All of the Mayor's daughters look different so I play many different characters."

Selena was definitely excited to work alongside some of the biggest names in comedy, and she was ready to show them what she could do. Unfortunately, the complicated recording schedules meant that Selena never actually met her on-screen dad, Steve Carell. They recorded in completely separate sessions, not that anyone can tell from the finished movie — it sounds like they were in the same room! Selena was a little disappointed. She had really been looking forward to meeting Steve. "It was kind of a bummer! But at the same time, it was cool. I can see him and say 'Hey, I played your daughter!'" Selena told the *New York Daily News*. Hopefully Selena will get the chance to act alongside Steve again — and this time actually come face-to-face with him!

The next role that Selena took on was much bigger. She won the lead part of Mary in *Another Cinderella Story*. It was the follow-up film to 2004's *A Cinderella Story* starring Disney alum Hilary Duff and *One Tree Hill*'s Chad Michael Murray. "It is not the sequel to the first one with Hilary Duff," Selena explained to the *New York Daily News*. Instead, it's another take on the same basic premise — a modern version of the Classic story of Cinderella. "At a ball, I meet a guy and we fall in love during a dance. Instead of dropping my glass slipper, I drop my

MP3 player." Mary, Selena's character, is a hip-hop and tango dancer, and over the course of the story she got to do some amazing dance sequences with her love interest in the film, Joey Parker. Andrew Seeley (Drew for short) played the part of Joey, and was best known as the singing voice for Zac Efron in Disney's *High School Musical*. He also co-wrote the Emmy nominated song, "Get'cha Head in the Game" from the film. With Andrew's great voice, natural charisma, and dance expertise, he was a natural fit for the role of Joey. Both Drew and Selena did some singing in the film, much to the delight of Selena's fans.

Selena's role in *Another Cinderella Story* was a little edgier than some of her other parts. She even got to have her first big on-screen romance. Mary and Joey develop a romantic relationship over the course of the film. Since Selena and Drew are just friends, it was challenging to fake that chemistry for the cameras. Selena was a little nervous about the kissing scene before they shot it.

Luckily, she and Drew became friends very quickly, and they had been filming together for weeks, so they were already pretty comfortable around each other by the time they shot that scene. "We haven't shot that [the kissing scene] yet, but I've been dancing with Drew for like three weeks. So I've known him really long. We've been rehearsing. It's so comfortable with him, so I don't think it's going to be too weird," Selena told *Girls' Life Magazine* before they had filmed the big scene. And according to Selenagomezweb.com, co-star Drew "had nothing but nice things to say about Selena: 'It was amazing, she's great. She's a lot of fun, knows not to take herself too seriously. That's the way I am, so we both had a lot of fun." And when Selena heard what he said, she added, "Awww, I love him. He's still my favorite co-star that I've ever worked with."

Filming romantic, flirty scenes with such a cutie was obviously a lot of fun for Selena. Mary was a very deep character, and the singing and challenging dance routines were an incredible part of the movie. Hopefully Selena will get more chances to showcase her many talents in the future!

Another Cinderella Story was supposed to be a feature film, but the studio decided to release it to DVD instead. Selena was disappointed, but she understood their decision. She knew it was purely a business choice since everyone who had worked on the film really believed in it. And the movie did get a special premiere when it aired for the first time on television on ABC Family in early 2009. ABC Family viewers loved it and Selena was excited to get a premiere — even if it was only on TV instead of in theaters!

With Selena's talent, she knew that there would be many other movies and premieres in her future! And she didn't have to wait very long for the next big opportunity to come along.

Axel Koester/Corbis

Selena and
David Henrie hit
the red carpet.

©Randy Holmes/Disney Channel/Retna Ltd.

Selena volunteering to plant trees with other Disney stars.

©Joel Warren/Disney Channel/Retna Ltd.

... and Miley on the set of *Hannah Montana.*

SELENA
rocking out!

Selena in **New York City.**

Selena poses with
a cute pooch!

Selena and Demi on the set of *Barney & Friends*.

This is Selena.

This is Demi.

Selena poses with her best friend Demi.

CHAPTER 8:
Princess Protection Program

Selena's fabulous real life friendship with Demi Lovato started during their early years, filming *Barney & Friends* together. Their friendship grew even stronger as they both landed roles in their own Disney Channel Original Series. While Selena was working on *Wizards of Waverly Place*, Demi was starring in the Disney made for television movie *Camp Rock*, recording her debut album, and shooting a pilot as Sonny in the Disney series *Sonny With a Chance*. Both girls were stars with successful careers, but Selena definitely missed acting and working with Demi. So, when Disney asked them to audition for different roles in the same movie, Selena was thrilled! Not surprisingly, their on-screen chemistry was as good as ever, and Selena and Demi were cast together in a new made-for-television Disney Channel Original Movie called *Princess Protection Program*. Selena won the part of girl-next-door Carter, and Demi was cast as Princess Rosalinda.

In the movie, when Princess Rosalinda's country is threatened with invasion by an evil dictator, she is rescued by the Princess Protection Program, a top-secret agency dedicated to the protection of princesses in peril. Rosalinda is sent to live with Mason, an agent in the program, in Louisiana. Mason has a teenage daughter named Carter, who he expects to help him keep Princess Rosalinda safe. So Rosalinda becomes Rosie, an ordinary teenager, and goes to school with Carter. Carter isn't happy to have to babysit a princess, and the two girls don't get along at first. Carter is insecure and a total tomboy. She pretends like she doesn't care about being popular, but she secretly dreams of dating her crush, Donnie, the cutest guy in town. Rosie fits right in at school and quickly becomes super popular, which only makes the two girls clash more. Eventually Carter teaches Rosie to be a normal teen and Rosie helps Carter learn to relax and be herself around the boy of her dreams. Selena told the Web site Just Jared Jr., "It's been like a dream come true. We did work together when we were younger, but then, we're best friends and we spend every second with each other. So, to be able to work with each other [again] was definitely one of our dreams."

Demi and Selena were very excited about filming the movie. They both had starring roles in a very well written script and they got to film together in tropical Puerto Rico for months! Selena and Demi have such busy schedules that they don't get to see each other as often as they would like. But, while filming, they had adjoining trailers and rooms in the same hotel, so they got to spend tons of time together. They were inseparable on and off set — practicing lines, doing homework, hanging out at the beach, and going surfing.

Selena also became good friends with the rest of the cast, including Samantha Droke, Jamie Chung, Robert Adamson, and Nicholas Braun. Samantha and Selena are old friends, even though Sam does play one of the mean girls in the film! The cast all enjoyed wearing tees from Sam's new clothing line that have her "Live in Love" logo across the front. There were also a number of actors from Puerto Rico in the cast and they showed Demi and Selena all the great local beaches and best spots to eat. Selena shared with TWIST magazine, "The cast is close. When we are done shooting, we'd hang out at the pool or go to dinner. We also went surfing!" It was definitely a fun set, so it was hard for Selena to say good-bye to everyone when filming ended. Even a super-fun wrap party on the beach with a bonfire, limbo contests, and lots of dancing didn't make it any easier. Luckily, a lot of the stars live in Los Angeles, so Selena knew they would stay in touch!

The movie premiered in June 2009 and Selena's fans loved it! It got rave reviews and it gave fans a chance to see Demi and Selena's BFF chemistry on-screen. It was such a hit that there could be a sequel, or maybe Disney will come up with another great project for Selena and Demi to do together soon.

CHAPTER 9:
Making Music

Selena is always going to be an actress, but she has an incredible voice and enjoys music, too. Her first musical experience was singing on *Barney & Friends*. Then a few years later, Selena recorded the song "Brain Zapped Theme Song" for the pilot episode of the television show *Brain Zapped*. Later, one of the talents that made her so popular with Disney Channel executives was her voice. As soon as she landed the role of Alex, Disney brought Selena into the studio to record the theme song for *Wizards of Waverly Place*. Selena had a blast recording "Everything Is Not What It Seems." It's a fun, upbeat pop song that gets stuck in fans' heads all the time! That was Selena's first very professional recording experience, and she learned a lot doing it. Recording a single isn't easy, especially for someone with very little experience. It was a lot of work, but by the end of the session, the song was perfect. It was pretty cool for Selena to hear herself singing that song and know that it would open her show!

Next Selena went back into the studio to record a cover of a classic Disney song, "Cruella De Vil." The original song is from the 1961 Disney animated movie *101 Dalmatians*, and it was the theme song of the movie's villainess, Cruella De Vil. It has always been a favorite of Disney fans. Selena's version has a really modern twist. It's very upbeat and totally fun to groove to!

To top off her "Cruella De Vil" recording, Selena filmed an awesome music video to go along with it! In the video, Selena sings on a fashion runway with her band behind her. Selena got to wear really cute clothes for the video, all in black, white, and red. She wore lots of polka-dots in the video to tie-in to the Dalmatian theme! The video was cut with scenes from the animated classic and with scenes of Selena singing alone in front of a black and white polka-dotted background. Getting to ham it up and sing for an audience was Selena's favorite part of recording the video. It gave her a real taste of what being a recording artist would be like. "I think you can be more of yourself when you're singing. You can have a little bit more control over it. It's a different process, with going into the studio and not having to worry about what you look like on camera. You write music and perform it, have fun, then go on concert and jam out in front of an audience," Selena told PBSKids.org.

Selena was very proud of the final product and fans loved it, too, when it aired on the Disney Channel! The video was also featured on the special, platinum edition *101 Dalmatians* DVD. And Selena's song was included in the *Disney Girlz Rock, Volume 2* CD and *Disneymania Volume 6*, the compilation CD that Disney puts out every year featuring hot new singers and bands covering classic songs.

Selena was getting really excited about recording music, and the opportunities just kept on coming! Selena laid down tracks for several songs for *Another Cinderella Story* next. The pop music was fun, hip hop infused, and perfect for dancing. She recorded "Tell Me Something I Don't Know" and "Bang a Drum." Selena and co-star Drew Seely also recorded the duet "New Classic" for the movie. Of course, Disney had other projects for her, too, so it wasn't long before Selena was headed back to the Disney Studios to record "Fly to your Heart," a new song for the new animated film *Tinker Bell.* Next, Selena and David Henrie recorded a song called "Make It Happen," which premiered in an episode of *Wizards of Waverly Place* in 2009!

Hollywood Records took notice of Selena's vocal talents and in 2008, just before Selena's sixteenth birthday, she signed a non-exclusive record deal with Hollywood

Records. Selena immediately went to work getting her band together and developing material to use for her debut album. "I would like all guys in the band," she laughed to *BOP Magazine*, "I'm looking for someone who's very passionate about music and can show me that they can rock out. I like having people with me to lean on and write with and have fun with." Selena is super excited to develop her own sound and share her love of music with her fans. "I want to do music that's fun. I don't want to do anything where people are like, 'Oh wow, she's trying to get too deep and serious.' I want to do something that everyone will jam out to."

Selena has so many friends in the music business that she'd like to record and perform with. She's hoping to go on tour with Demi Lovato in the summer of 2009. She also shared with AceShowbiz.com that she'd love to work with Taylor Swift in the near future, adding that the girls have already chatted about it. "We have talked about a duet," Selena explained. "I think it would be really neat to have the country vibe." She also confided to *Popstar!* that she'd like to work with Taylor because she "is not just plain country, [but] she's got a little pop edge to her. It's something I really admire, so we want to write a really awesome country-rock song and it sounds a little weird but we're totally down for that." Selena also recently worked with one of her favorite bands from Texas — Forever The Sickest Kids. She added vocals to one of their songs, "She's a Lady." They blogged about her visit on their official Web site, "We got a surprise visit today at the studio by a very special lady, Selena came by to hang, she is so super fun and one of the most talented, down to earth friends we have met. . . . We just had the most rockin' time ever with her and are pulling super hard for her and her new album!" No matter who Selena works with, the result is always amazing!

Of course, Selena has very particular ideas about who she wants to be as a singer. She's seen what other Disney stars have done with their recording careers, and wants to try something different. "I'm going to be in a band — no Selena Gomez stuff," she told MTV News. "I'm not going to be a solo artist. . . . I will be singing, and I'm learning drums and playing electric guitar. . . . I basically want to make music that is fun and that parents and kids can jump around to and have a good time to." "Once I come out with my music, you're going to see a whole different side of me. Different hair, different clothing, different attitude," Selena confessed to *Us* magazine .com. In her publicity photo for Hollywood Records, posted on their Web site, Selena is sporting an edgy new look with smoky makeup and a wind blown hair style. Selena hopes her fans will love her music as much as she does. "Most of my songs are about love," Selena posted on her blog. "I am a sixteen-year-old teenager, and I sing about what is on every girl's mind, love." Love is right, since Selena's fans are sure to love her album!

CHAPTER 10:
Rising Star

Selena is a star with a very bright future indeed. She has already established herself as an incredible actress, dancer, and singer — and there is tons more to come! She has already been hard at work in the recording studios of Hollywood Records, laying down tracks for her debut album. Selena told *Variety* that, "Music is another of my passions. I'm working on my first album for Hollywood Records. It'll be fun dance music, out next summer, and I'll be doing a national tour." She has been working very hard to perfect her sound and the final result will feature Selena with a cool back-up band if Selena gets her way. She really wants the band to play a big role in the album, much like her favorite group Paramore, which is a band of three guys with a female lead singer! The more she records, the more excited Selena becomes about getting her music out to fans. "Hopefully I'll finish up in April and debut my album in July," Selena told UsMagazine.com. "I'm really excited that people will see a whole other side of me." Selena would love for her album to come out in time for her to go on tour with her best friend Demi Lovato!

As for acting, Selena will continue playing Alex on *Wizards of Waverly Place* until the series ends. She absolutely loves her show, especially since it doesn't film year-round, so Selena has plenty of free time to pursue other acting gigs. "I love being challenged," Selena told UsMagazine.com. "I love the Disney channel, and I always want to keep that relationship because they gave me my start, but I'd love to someday make a transition and do roles that are really challenging for me. I'd like to do comedy, romance, anything." Selena is very focused on expanding her acting skills with more film roles. Selena is being very picky about which roles she accepts because she does not want to get locked in to a specific stereotype. "Workwise, my role model is Rachel McAdams. I fell in love with her in the movie *Mean Girls*, I love how she spreads herself out. She did a teen movie, a romance, a comedy, a family movie, a thriller. She reinvents herself each time, and that's what I respect and love about her the most," Selena explained to PBSKids. org. Selena is definitely on the right path to becoming the next Rachel McAdams. She can do comedy, drama, and even voice-over work without breaking a sweat, so her future possibilities are really limitless!

New projects are presented to Selena every day, and she has one coming up that she is very excited about. Selena was cast as big-sister Beezus in the upcoming movie, *Ramona and Beezus*, an adaptation of Beverly Cleary's popular *Ramona* children's book series. Ramona will be played by up-and-coming child actress, Joey King.

The movie will also star Ginnifer Goodwin as the girls' favorite aunt, Aunt Bea; and John Corbett and Bridget Moynahan as the two girls' parents, Dorothy and Bob Quimby. The movie will be directed by Elizabeth Allen.

Selena's character, Beezus, is neat, studious, responsible, and above all, sensible, while little sister Ramona is accident-prone, rambunctious, and always getting into trouble. Although Beezus is frequently annoyed with Ramona (and vice versa), she takes care of her little sister, defending and supporting her when needed. Shooting started in April 2009, and was filmed on location in Vancouver, British Columbia, Canada. The movie release date is set for spring 2010, but isn't final yet. Selena blogged about the flick on her MySpace Page, "I wanted to share with you guys that as soon as I get done here in Puerto Rico, I will be heading off [to] my second favorite place in the world — Vancouver, Canada! I spent three months there last year [shooting *Another Cinderella Story*] and now I will be spending another couple of months there shooting *Ramona*! I can't wait to go back! So, if you live in Canada, I can't wait to see you guys!! Hope you're all doing well! God Bless, Sel." *Ramona and Beezus* is just the type of film Selena was hoping to work on next. With its star-studded cast, family-friendly message, and complex characters, Selena knows working on *Ramona and Beezus* will help her grow and develop as an actress — and she knows her fans will love it, too!

When it comes to choosing other types of characters to play in the future, Selena is really open to anything. Although, there are a few parts Selena would love to sink her teeth into! "I'd like to play a mean girl. I did play a mean girl on *Hannah Montana*, but I'd like to be the bad person in a movie. Just something different to challenge myself!", Selena told PBSKids.org. Selena has gotten a little tired of waiting for great roles to come to her. So Selena and her mom decided to get into the feature film business themselves. Selena's production company, July Moon Productions, is looking for great feature films to produce that Selena can star in. "I'll have my own control of my career and what my movie decisions will be," Selena told E! Online. "I want to make sure I choose roles that will challenge me as an actress." Selena is very excited about the possibility of producing a film as well as starring in it. She's had a lot of experience over the past few years and is hoping to bring some fresh, new ideas to her work behind the camera.

Of course, Selena will probably continue to guest star on Disney shows. She already made a big splash on *The Suite Life of Zack & Cody* and *Hannah Montana*, and even made an appearance in a Jonas Brothers music video for the song "Burnin' Up." She would love to guest star on Demi Lovato's new series *Sonny With a Chance* and would definitely be up to working with the Jonas Brothers again on their new show, *J.O.N.A.S!* One thing for sure, Selena will probably be working with Disney for a long time to come. Selena is so happy that Disney executives have given her the chance to do what she loves every single day, and she is very proud of all of the work she has done with Disney. Plus, there will be plenty of time for more adult roles in the future — for now Selena can just enjoy being a kid! It will be fun for her fans to follow the career of this charming young starlet as she spreads her wings to fly!

CHAPTER 11:
Backstage Pass

Selena might be a big star these days, but when she's at home she's just a regular girl. Her mom, Mandy and step-dad, Brian, expect Selena to help around the house and do her chores just like her fans do! Mandy told *People*, "She has to do her own laundry. If she cooks, I clean. If I cook, she cleans. She has to help feed the dogs. There are really no set chores. We just all pitch in when needed. . . . Selena knows who she is, and I am around to make sure she doesn't change."

Selena's parents are very serious about making sure she has the supervision and the support she needs. They want her to be successful, but her happiness and well-being are always the most important things to them. "My mom is my best friend. She's always with me everywhere I go. Sometimes on set, I just need to see her face. I'm like, 'Mom, I need to see you.' I just have to have my mom," Selena explained to *Girls' Life Magazine*. She admits her mother's strength has inspired her to go after her dreams and remain on a successful path. My role model is "first and foremost my mom. I grew up watching *Wizard of Oz* and 'Somewhere Over the Rainbow' was the first song I learned to sing," Selena laughingly told *Variety*. A dedicated and loving mother? Not a bad role model at all!

Selena doesn't get to see her dad and her extended family as much as she wants to because she is busy filming for various projects, traveling to appearances, or working in the recording studio. But she takes any chance she gets to go home to Texas. Selena is a sentimental girl at heart who always puts her family and friends first when she can. She always makes sure she gets to spend holidays with her family, and looks forward to those visits all year. She explained to MSN.com, "This will be the first year that I'll be able to go home since I moved away from Texas, so I'll be spending the holidays with my family on my dad's side and my mom's side and coming back to Texas for a good two weeks and doing nothing, which is very refreshing." Selena gets pretty homesick when she goes too long between visits, as she revealed to *Tiger Beat* magazine. "I think about home a lot. I don't get to go home to Texas often. I miss my family. They're the reason I am the person I am today." Luckily, Selena's family is very understanding. They all know how much she loves them and how important they are to her even if she doesn't get to see them as much as she would like. With e-mail and lots of phone calls, they keep in touch pretty regularly when she can't make a trip home.

There are a few more important family members that Selena always makes time for — her dogs! Selena has always loved animals and her dogs are an important part of the family. "My family has four dogs — and there's a great trail by our house where we love to take them hiking!" Selena told Hollyscoop.com. Selena has even gotten involved with a charity in Puerto Rico to help homeless dogs and cats there. Selena filmed a "Dog-umentary" about all of the stray animals out on the streets of Puerto Rico and has joined forces with Charity Buzz to benefit Island Dog, Inc. She has blogged about her new pet project and encouraged fans to donate money to the great charity.

Except for her family, there is no one Selena wants to spend time with more than her BFF, Demi Lovato. Selena and Demi don't get to see each other as much as they did growing up, so they make the most of every minute they do get to spend together these days. They talk about clothes, their ideas and experiences, and of course, boys! Selena and Demi love to share their lives with their fans, too. They spend a lot of time recording videos together for their YouTube site and keeping up with their Facebook and MySpace pages. Selena's friendship with Demi has lasted so long, in part, because each girl understands exactly where the other is coming from. They have a lot in common, including acting, music, shopping, skateboarding, and surfing. So they always have plenty to do and talk about when they're together! And they always manage to keep in touch when they're apart with e-mails, texts, phone calls, and Twitter!

Even when Selena and Demi can't get together very often, they always have each other's backs. Selena told *Girls' Life Magazine*, "My best girl friend would be Demi Lovato, and she's from Texas as well. I actually met her when I did *Barney & Friends* when I was about seven. We both did that show together, and now . . . we're still best friends. Now she's off working for [the] Disney Channel [the Jonas Brothers' *Camp Rock*]. It's almost weird. My best guy bud is Randy Hill and he's still back in Texas, working at a skate shop. I can always go to him when I need someone to talk to." Both Randy and Demi often turn to Selena for advice. Selena's logical approach to things always helps her friends out. "He [Randy] always asks me about stuff. He's like, 'Well, I'm going on a date with this girl. Hey can I wear this?' I laugh at him. I'm like, 'Yeah, you can wear that. It should be fine.' He'll ask me about what he should get a girl for a present and stuff like that," Selena explained to *Girls' Life Magazine*. Of course, Randy and Demi are both always happy to return the favor and give Selena advice when she's in a bind. Having best friends that she's known since childhood has been very important to Selena. She can completely relax away from the spotlight with them and be as goofy and silly as she wants. Plus, they never let Selena get away with any diva-like behavior since they knew her before she was a star! Selena can't imagine her life without her best friends to remind her of who she really is. Her BFF, Demi, is especially important to Selena now that they are both in Los Angeles living their dreams. "We're going through the madness together. Thank goodness," she confessed to Maggie Rodriguez on *The Early Show*, "I'm so blessed and I'm so happy that she's there because you meet a lot of people that you may not be able to trust, so I'm happy that I have her."

So what do Selena and Demi do when they get together? "I unwind by having movie nights with friends. I love nineties horror movies — they're more funny than scary," Selena told Hollyscoop.com. She also loves movies starring her celebrity crushes! "My celebrity crush is, oh, what is his name? He was in *Alpha Dog* and *Into the Wild.* Emile Hirsch," Selena told *Girls' Life Magazine.* "It was Shia LaBeouf, then I saw a couple of movies with Emile Hirsch, and I was like, 'I have a new crush.' He's so cute." Selena would love to star in a movie with either of those stars as her love interest! "It's very far-fetched, but I would love to have Shia on *Wizards,*" Selena confided to UsMagazine.com. It might not be as far-fetched as Selena thinks. When he was younger, Shia starred on the Disney Channel as Louis Stevens on the series *Even*

Stevens and he played the lead role of Stanley Yelnats IV in the Disney feature film *Holes*. Shia would probably love to come back to Disney for a guest appearance!

You won't find Selena snacking on nachos or candy while watching her favorite flicks. Instead you might find her snacking on a nice, crunchy pickle. "I just love pickles, I guess I'm a sour girl," Selena told *Girls' Life Magazine*. Where Selena grew up in Texas, she could buy pickles in movie theaters! Selena loves pickles so much that when she visited *Ellen* in January 2008, Ellen DeGeneres gave Selena a pair of special Converse sneakers that she drew pickles on! But pickles are just the beginning of Selena's odd snacking habits. She also loves to eat lemons sprinkled with salt! "It actually started when I did *Barney*. At lunch, my friend Demi and a bunch of other castmates would put sugar on their lemons, but I didn't like it. It was too sweet. So I put salt on it, and I fell in love with it ever since," Selena told *Girls' Life Magazine*. Selena eats lemons almost every day, and sometimes it really grosses out her friends. "[Maria Canals Barrera] who plays my mom on the show — she says, 'How can you eat a whole lemon?' She always says, 'It's because you're from Texas, that's why.' She always laughs at me, but I love lemons. I just have a whole lemon and put a little salt on it. My mom is getting on me for that because it's bad for my teeth. But I'm like, 'I brush every day, every night,' and she's like, 'It doesn't matter. It's going to get your enamel.' She's getting all mad at me," Selena told *Girls' Life Magazine*. Of course a good snack wouldn't be complete without a yummy drink. Selena's fav is "Sugar-free Red Bull! I had a sip of my mom's and I was like, 'Oooh, this is good!' but she won't let me have too many. But every now and then, if I have a meeting or something, she'll let me. It gives me a little jolt of energy so I can focus on work or something!" Selena explained to *Popstar!*

Selena has a lot of friends in addition to her two best friends. Selena hangs out with her *Wizards of Waverly Place* co-stars all the time. An only child, Selena says that

David Henrie and Jake T. Austin "have become like my real brothers. By that I mean we fight and argue, too," she told the Associated Press. "We do the whole, like, picking on each other brotherly-sister thing." Selena grew up with a large extended family in Texas and her friends in Los Angeles have become a second family to her. "We text each other as soon as we leave set. We ask our parents, 'Can we go to the mall? Can we go to the movies?'"

Jen, David, Jake, and Selena all like to go surfing, too. Selena and her friends see surfing as a way to let loose and relieve stress. That's probably a great feeling for the busy stars. Selena explained to *Discovery Girls*, "My idea of getting away is going surfing. . . . I've surfed six hours in one day!" Selena spilled to *BOP Magazine*, "Now that I live in Los Angeles, my favorite place to spend the summer is the beach. We didn't have that in Dallas. I like to surf in Malibu, sometimes with the cast of *Wizards of Waverly Place*. Jake T. Austin, who plays my younger brother on the show, taught me how to surf.

I'm addicted to it." Selena has gotten a lot of her friends into surfing, including Demi, who also likes skateboarding with Selena.

Selena has lots of guy friends and she's a very pretty girl, so its no surprise that there have been lots of rumors about who she might be dating. But Selena is single, and isn't in any hurry to be in a serious relationship. "No, actually I do not [have a boyfriend]. I don't. I'm traveling right now, . . . I don't really think I necessarily need one now, and I'm not at home. I'm not in California. I'm in Canada, so I'll be here for a while. So maybe around next year I'll have one then, but not right now. I'm focusing on work and school," Selena told *Girls' Life Magazine*. Selena's name has been linked to her *Wizard* co-stars David Henrie and Jake T. Austin, as well as with crooning cutie Nick Jonas. Selena did make an appearance in the Jonas Brothers' "Burnin' Up" video, visited Demi Lovato when she was on tour with the Jonas Brothers, and has become good friends with all the Jonas brothers. But, Selena told

UsMagazine.com that she and Nick Jonas are just getting to know each other. "I've gotten really close to the entire Jonas family this past year. Nick and I are getting to know each other, but we're not confirming anything." Selena also told *People* magazine she was unattached. "Of course, boys are on every girl's mind. . . . I don't think I need a boyfriend right now. I have crushes and I go on dates . . . but younger kids my age take that stuff way too seriously." Selena may be interested in someone in particular, but she's keeping her lips sealed. For Selena, romance is private. She wouldn't want a boy to kiss her and then tell everyone about it, so she keeps quiet, too. Selena is known for wearing a purity ring. It's a personal commitment for her that she doesn't talk about often. But even so, some people have made mean comments about her ring. Selena told PopEater.com how weird the criticism is, "It's something I made a promise to myself, to my family, and to God . . . people say, 'She's trying too hard.' I'm not trying to be anybody but myself." Luckily,

Selena never lets criticism get to her. She knows that she's being true to herself and doesn't let anyone make her feel bad about that.

Selena is confident, successful, and has every right to be proud of her many accomplishments. She has a wonderful supportive family and many fun, creative friends she enjoys spending time with. In the end, Selena is as caring and down-to-earth now as she was the day she came to Hollywood from Texas. She owes that to the many genuine friendships she has that keep her from getting carried away in the fast-paced entertainment world. So whether she is goofing around watching movies, skateboarding, or surfing, Selena will always make the most of her time with her good friends and loving family!

CHAPTER 12:
Giving Back

Giving back to her community and using her popularity to increase awareness for causes that are important to her are high on Selena's list of priorities. "I'm very happy that I have a voice, and I'm going to use it," Selena told *Scholastic News* about her involvement in charities and other public service organizations. Selena knows she has been blessed with a successful career, a loving family, and a safe home, but she also knows that not everyone is as lucky as she is. So she always makes time in her busy schedule to contribute her money, time, and voice to causes that are important to her.

One of the most important charities that Selena is a part of is the AmberWatch Foundation. It is an organization that helps educate kids and their parents about keeping kids safe from predators, and Selena is the new Youth Coalition chairperson. Selena is in charge of reaching out to other young people and getting them to volunteer. It's very important to have youth involvement, since kids often confide in their friends instead of their parents when they are in trouble. On the Web site of AmberWatchFoundation.org, Selena says, "I am honored to take on the role of chair of the AmberWatch Foundation Youth Coalition and look forward to working closely with the Foundation's members to promote education and help empower children to avoid dangerous situations." Selena wants to make sure every child knows how to keep himself safe in every situation. She also works with other young volunteers at events and to brainstorm new ideas to help prevent child abductions.

In the fall of 2008, Selena was named the youngest ever spokesperson for the Trick-or-Treat for UNICEF campaign. She told *Seventeen* magazine how excited she was about the honor. "I was recently competing for UNICEF's [2008 Trick-or-Treat campaign] spokesperson, and I freaked out when I got that!" It was the 58th anniversary of the United Nations Children's Fund event. The Trick-or-Treat campaign encourages children in America to make Halloween really count by collecting money instead of candy to benefit other children around the world. "I am extremely excited to be this year's Trick-or-Treat for UNICEF spokesperson," Selena said in a UNICEF press release. "I want to help encourage other kids to make a difference in the world and show them that Trick-or-Treat for UNICEF is such a great, fun way to get involved." Selena always participated in the UNICEF Trick or Treat campaign when she was growing up. "I loved those little boxes I would get in school [on Halloween] to go get money for kids. It's a great cause," Selena said to *Seventeen* magazine. These days, Selena doesn't get to do much trick-or-treating, but she gets all of her family and friends to donate instead!

A month later, during the 2008 presidential election, Selena became involved with UR Votes Count, a nationwide campaign devoted to educating teens on the importance of voting. She feels it is important for kids to understand the political process. "I'm sixteen now, but in two years, I'll have the opportunity to vote. It's kind of a scary thought to think that in four years, I will be voting for the person that will have to run my country for me, and I want to be prepared for that." Selena talks to her family about politics, elections, and the issues that are important to them. She told *Seventeen* magazine, "The economy is important to me and my family right now. Education and global warming are big issues for me as well. . . . I think that it's actually kind of fun to discuss it with my parents when we're eating dinner or watching TV because I get to learn what they have to say and how their thought process works." All of the issues raised around a big election can get confusing — especially since both candidates sincerely believe that they can help the country the most. UR Votes Count helps kids understand the issues and clarifies exactly where each side stands objectively. Selena definitely found that helpful to clarify how she felt about each candidate.

Selena gets into discussions about issues and the candidates with her friends, as she told to *Seventeen* magazine, "Demi [Lovato] and I can go for hours on issues like that. If you make one comment about *any* candidate, we will sit there for two hours, three hours, arguing. Sometimes we'll walk away angry at each other, but we'll just laugh about it later." Selena really enjoyed her experience encouraging other kids to get involved with the presidential election. "I think that a lot of celebrities are getting involved this year, so I think that gets people excited. . . . It's just amazing to have kids come up to me saying they made a group night with all their girl-friends and watched the presidential debates together!

It's incredible to know that I can have that kind of impact on someone," she added to *Seventeen* magazine. "Don't stop yourself from being educated. If you like the person who is running the country, I think you should watch how they run it, to the point where you will be able to vote for the next president." Selena definitely wants teens to stay informed about politics to make sure they still have a voice.

In the spring of 2009, Selena lent her voice to a new cause that she felt was in line with her overall goal of helping kids and teens stay safe. Selena filmed two Public Service Announcements for State Farm Insurance aimed at helping young drivers stay safe behind the wheel and reduce the number of fatal car crashes every year. In the first video, Selena is "driving" a hot, red convertible and tells her mom, "I'm learning a lot about being a safe driver, too. . . . I don't text or talk on the phone while I'm driving, never have too many friends in the car, and I always wear my seat belt." Selena, along with her mom,

Mandy, in the passenger seat, filmed the commercial in front of a green screen and then a beautiful countryside was added in the background during editing. In the second video, Selena is on the *Wizards* set and shares what she's learned about driving, saying, "Being a safe driver means not taking any chances. Always wear your seat belt and pay attention to the speed limit. And don't text or talk on the phone while driving. Who doesn't love to text? But I can wait." Selena also credits her mom Mandy with teaching her safe driving. "I have a really good teacher," she says in the commercial. "Thanks Mom." These spots aired on the Disney Channel.

Teen driver safety is especially important to Selena since she recently became old enough to drive. Selena got her learner's permit when she was sixteen and practiced as much as she could to prep for her driver's test. Her stepfather taught her how to signal, merge, and parallel park in her Ford Escape Hybrid because "my mom's too scared to teach me!" Selena joked to *People* magazine.

Selena isn't nervous about driving but says she'll have to make some sacrifices when it comes to her BlackBerry. She explained to *People,* "I'm going to try to put my phone on silent. You can tell yourself, 'I'm not going to get it,' but once you hear it you get tempted and distracted. So for me . . . I'll put it on silent, put it in my purse and just drive. . . . I've almost been in wrecks because of people [using phones while driving]. I'll sit there and look at someone and go, 'Gosh! She completely almost ran into us,' then look at her and see she's on the phone. That's the reason! . . . In the car, just focus on what you need to be doing." Luckily for everyone on the road in Los Angeles, Selena is a very safe and responsible driver and hopefully her encouragement is inspiring other teens to be safe, too!

In addition to teen safety, one of Selena's most important interests is the environment. Ecology has always been Selena's favorite subject, as she explained to *Girls' Life Magazine,* "I have no idea why, but there's something

116

about learning about our planet and everything else, even the specific things like learning about flowers or something. I really love it." Lately, Selena has been learning a lot about the dangers that pollution and global warming pose, and its really inspired her to get involved. She told *Scholastic News*, "I'm learning about global warming and stuff like that. I've actually cried about this stuff because it's awful that it's happening. But I encourage everyone to help with that. My mom and I want to help and we donate and anything else we can do. I think it's really important to do whatever we can." Protecting the ocean and beaches is especially important to Selena since she loves surfing so much! Even when Selena doesn't have time in her busy schedule to do big things to help the environment, she makes sure she does the little things that help every day. "We just want to do as much as possible. We recycle, we do everyday little things that people don't think will matter. But in reality, those little things are the most important. Doing everything you can and spreading the word," she told *Girls' Life Magazine*. Selena would want her fans to do those little things too — like recycling, using less water, and turning off lights when you leave a room!

While Selena was in Puerto Rico filming the *Wizards of Waverly Place: The Movie*, she decided to join DoSomething.org and help feed stray puppies! She posted a message to her fans on her MySpace blog saying, "I'm honored to be the new ambassador for DoSomething.org! The last time I was in PR [Puerto Rico] shooting *Princess Protection Program* we noticed all of these stray dogs and puppies. We ended up finding out that Puerto Rico has a 'dead dog beach.' It sounds worse than it is, but people actually kill dogs for fun here. This time around I'm teaming up with DoSomething.org and my mom, Brian, David, Jake, David D are all going to help out today along with some of my crew from set! We are spending the day feeding puppies, washing them and hanging out with them. After we spend the day with them we are sending these dogs to different places in the U.S., the no-kill dog shelters so they can find a home." Selena has four dogs herself, so saving animals from neglect and abuse will always be an important cause for her!

Selena is asked to make a lot of public appearances, too. She presents awards, attends premieres and concerts, and goes to media events promoting worthy organizations. Selena is happy to attend, especially when the event is for a good cause! She especially enjoys all the cool promotional activities and special events that Disney comes up with for their stars! Selena and her co-stars from *Wizards of Waverly Place* hosted Disney Channel's 2008 New Year's Eve television event, and she competed in the 2008 Disney Channel Games. The Games gave fans a chance to see their favorite stars strut their athletic stuff, and the winning team got to donate $100,000 to the charity of their choice. Selena was on the yellow team, captained by Kevin Jonas, and was a strong competitor. Selena's team didn't win, but she had a lot of fun competing for a good cause!

Selena's life is a whirlwind of work and activities these days, but she has always been willing to take the time to support her favorite charities and to use her star power to stand up for what she believes in. She hopes that her willingness to get involved and take a stand will inspire her fans to get involved, too!

CHAPTER 13:
Stylin' with Selena

Selena is well known for her laid-back, sporty-chic fashion look. She pairs sporty pieces with more girly touches and accessories to get her trademark flirty, casual style. Her wardrobe is full of skinny pants, graphic T-shirts, chunky jewelry, vests, bright colors, and, of course, Converse! Selena told PBSKids.org, "I'm a huge Converse girl. I think I have about twenty pairs in different colors." Selena definitely has a pair of Converse sneakers to match any outfit. And she needs all of those options, since she loves to experiment with bright colors. For casual days out, Selena pairs skinny jeans with boots and long printed tops or slouchy sweaters. Selena gets her so-cute style by mixing new clothes with vintage finds! "I love thrift shops!" she tells *BOP Magazine*. "I'm a huge bargain shopper!" Selena always looks cute, but it is definitely important to her that her outfits are fun and easy to move around in — just in case she wants to play a pick-up basketball game or chase her television brothers around the set. "I can't dress in something I'm not comfortable in," Selena told PBSKids.org. Selena's insistence on comfort is probably why she always looks confident and happy — even on the red carpet!

Selena has really been getting into amping up her style when she has to walk the red carpet or attend an event or premiere. In fact, the starlet has been expanding her style, dressing up more and liking it! She often wears metallic heels or sandals with dark, skinny jeans and cute, embellished tops to events. And for the red carpet, Selena pulls out all the stops. She favors simple dresses in bold colors with unique cuts — like one-shoulder gowns! Selena loves BCBG and other designers and she told

OK! magazine, "I started out as a tomboy, but over the past year my wardrobe's gotten classier. I'm growing up." Selena knows her look will change and evolve over time, and she believes that the important thing isn't what she wears, it's the way that she wears it. "Self-confidence is a huge part of it. You can't think that you're not as good as anyone else. And I think it's important to be careful of what you do and say and who you hang out with. Represent yourself well, even in the clothes you wear," Selena explained to PBSKids.org.

Selena has been taking her style to extremes for her interviews in a couple of well-known magazines. On her *Latina* magazine cover, Selena is dressed in a brilliant canary-yellow strapless dress. Inside the magazine, she was photographed wearing some fun and funky Tex-Mex style western wear, chunky jewelry, and cowboy boots. She told Latina.com, "My favorite part of the photo shoot today, it was very different, a kind of western look. It was very neat to be able to be kinda more daring with my clothing." And in a recent *OK!* magazine spread, Selena is modeling a variety of updated looks, including an animal print top with a short hair style, a flowing, flirty dress, a striped nautical top with jeans and cap, and a preppy slack-and-sweater set with heels and an up-do. It is definitely a more grown-up, classic teenage look. But Selena's favorite was probably the sultry rocker, wind-blown look, with a metallic jacket and short denim skirt!

No matter what she wears, Selena always finishes off her look with the perfect accessories. She is really into funky jewelry, and she owns tons of bracelets, necklaces, and big earrings. But shoes are Selena's favorite thing to shop for. Shoes can really make or break an outfit, and Selena has tons of shoes to choose from. She has every kind of shoe imaginable — boots, pumps, peep-toe wedges, flat sandals, kitten heels, and lots of sneakers. Her collection would make any girl jealous!

Makeup and hair are also a big part of Selena's signature style. Selena usually wears very light, natural makeup — just a little bronzer, blush, mascara, and lip gloss for every day. Of course, for a glamorous event, Selena will add some darker lip gloss and some fun eye shadow and eyeliner. Selena's long, layered, dark hair is very versatile. She can pin it up to make it look shorter, straighten it for a sleek look, let it fall in soft waves, or pull it back in a sporty ponytail or messy bun. With so many options, Selena's hair lets her change up her look all the time.

Selena's style is definitely inspiring, and the stylists on *Wizards of Waverly Place* took notice. They based Alex's style on the show after Selena's real life looks. Alex is even more of a tomboy than Selena is, so they dress her in lots of jeans, sporty tops, and sneakers! "I wear the Converse and Vans and funky tops and chunky jewelry, but I don't get in trouble as much as she [Alex] does!" Selena laughed to *Teen* magazine. Of course, there are definite perks to playing a stylish character on TV. Selena loves getting dressed for filming every day, especially since she gets to keep some of the clothes when they are done with them! The crew shops for Alex at stores like Urban Outfitters, Forever 21, and Wet Seal where they can find fun prints, bright colors, and lots of layering pieces and cool accessories. Selena even has a say in Alex's wardrobe from time to time. "Wardrobe would always talk to me and get ideas from the clothes I'd wear to the set. Now my character wears nothing but Converse! That's so fun for me because I get to wear different Converse all the time," Selena told *DiscoveryGirls*.

Both Selena and Alex have great style, so it's no wonder that fans love to copy their looks. "I'm usually so casual. But little girls have come up to me, and they show me that they dress like me. A girl brought me a picture and said, 'I dressed up like you for school,' and it almost made me cry," she told *Girls' Life Magazine*. Imitation is definitely okay with Selena — and most of her fans can copy her look with things they already have in their closets. If you feel like looking like Selena, try pairing your favorite skinny jeans with Converse sneakers, hoop earrings, a printed tank top, and a cool scarf. Or slip into a one-shoulder dress and metallic kitten heels to head out for the night. Of course, the best way to nab Selena's style is to copy her confidence. As long as you feel great in what you're wearing, you will look just as fab as she always does!

CHAPTER 14:
Just the Facts

FULL NAME: Selena Marie Gomez

NICKNAME: Sel

BIRTH DATE: July 22, 1992

STAR SIGN: Cancer

HOMETOWN: Grand Prairie, Texas

HEIGHT: 5'5"

HAIR COLOR: Dark Brown

EYE COLOR: Brown

PARENTS: mom Mandy Teefey and stepdad Brian
Teefey,
dad Ricardo Gomez

SIBLINGS: None

BEST FRIENDS: Demi Lovato, Randy Hill

128

CELEB CRUSH: Shia LaBeouf, Emile Hirsch

FAVORITE THANKSGIVING FOOD: Stuffing

FAVORITE PIZZA TOPPINGS: Cheese, mushrooms, jalapeño peppers

FAVORITE SNACKS: Dill pickles, lemons with salt

FAVORITE COMFORT FOOD: Cookie dough

FAVORITE FRUIT: Mangoes

FAVORITE SUBJECT: Biology

FAVORITE COSMETICS: Carmex lip balm, Cover Girl Wet Slicks lip gloss, MAC's Naked Lunch eye shadow

FAVORITE TV SHOW: *Gossip Girl*

FAVORITE MOVIE: *The Wizard of Oz*

FAVORITE ACTRESS: Rachel McAdams

HOBBIES: Painting, drawing, singing, surfing, skateboarding, basketball

FAVORITE BAND: Paramore

PETS: Four dogs

CHAPTER 15:
Selena Online

Want more Selena? Here is a list of extremely cool and interesting Web sites that have tons of information on Selena Gomez. If you want to find out what she's been doing, saying, or wearing, these are the sites to visit!

You can do a lot of cool stuff on the Internet, like play games, chat with friends, or even watch your favorite episodes of *Wizards of Waverly Place*. One really fun thing to do is watch her funny YouTube videos that Selena makes with her friends and co-stars from her shows, telling her fans and friends about all of her fun activities. But Selena would always want you to be careful when you are hanging out online. Always get your parents permission to surf the web. And never try to meet someone in person that you met online or give out any sort of personal information, like your name, address, phone number, or the name of your school or sports team.

Don't worry if your fav Selena Web site disappears. Web sites come and go, but there's sure to be plenty of good Web sites about a star like Selena!

www.selenagomez.com

This is Selena's official website that has it all—the latest music, photos, and messages from Selena to her fans, and some of her YouTube videos along with links to her other official sites.

www.myspace.com/selenagomez

This is Selena's official MySpace page with her updated blog.

CHAPTER 16:
Quiztastic!

You are obviously a huge Selena fan, but do you know which of her characters you would be most like? She's played a lot of different roles — and all of them were totally awesome! But are you an Alex, Carter, Mary, or a Mikayla? Take the quiz below to find out!

1. You have a few hours free after school. How do you spend them?

   a. making nachos and watching sports

   b. playing practical jokes on your siblings

   c. coming up with plans to boost your popularity

   d. hitting the dance studio to get in a few hours of practice

   e. surfing at the beach

2. You have a huge crush on a guy, how do you get his attention?

a. You ask if you can join his football game

b. You convince him that you are his lucky charm

c. You call him and tell him he's taking you out

d. You leave him subtle clues and hope he notices!

e. You hang out with him at the skate park for some no-pressure flirting

3. Your favorite chill out activity is:

a. fishing

b. watching movies in Central Park

c. getting a manicure

d. listening to your Zune music player

e. watching a movie with friends

4. Life isn't all fun. You have responsibilities that include:

a. working at your after school job

b. special after school classes

c. answering your fan mail

d. taking care of your demanding family members

e. walking the family dogs

5. You best friend is:

a. a total princess

b. funny — with totally wacky fashion sense

c. your manager

d. a girl from your dance class

e. a talented girl you grew up with

6. You would describe yourself best as:

a. a tomboy

b. a troublemaker

c. a superstar

d. a dancer

e. well-rounded and driven

7. You love to give back to your community! What's your favorite cause?

  a. Raising money for hurricane victims

  b. Helping older residents in your neighborhood with day-to-day activities

  c. United People's Relief Charity

  d. Raising money for scholarships for deserving students

  e. Helping homeless puppies

Now count up your answers and see which of Selena's characters fits you best!

If you chose mostly A's then you are most like Carter from *Princess Protection Program*! You are a total tomboy, but you don't always want to be just one of the guys. In fact, you'd love it if more guys paid attention to you! You are funny, sarcastic, and very chill. You love the great outdoors and never worry too much about getting dirty or messy. You are a lot of fun to hang out with and your friends all appreciate your laid-back attitude.

If you chose mostly B's then you are most like Alex Russo from *Wizards of Waverly Place*. Your motto is "rules are made to be broken!" It's not that you mean to cause trouble, you just can't help yourself. You love practical jokes and giving your siblings a hard time. You do like to help people, but it doesn't always turn out as planned. Luckily, your friends and family always know that you mean well! You are funny, loyal, and great at coming up with plans to bend the rules or get around things — which definitely comes in handy! You are the go-to girl if a friend needs help getting out of a tough situation. Your buds all love you because you always lead them on fun and exciting adventures — a night out with you is never boring!

If you chose mostly C's then you are most like popstar Mikayla from *Hannah Montana*. You are a super star in the making — and you know it! You love to be the center of attention and you don't mind stepping up and grabbing the spotlight. Of course, you are always happy to share it with your best friends! You definitely have the drive and determination to succeed. All you have to do is keep working to make your dreams come true. You are favorite with friends for parties because you know just how to get a crowd warmed up and you are always the first one on the dance floor.

If you chose mostly D's then you are most like Mary Santiago from *Another Cinderella Story*. You definitely have the talent and determination to make your dreams come true — you just have to step into the spotlight. You have a tendency to be a little shy or quiet, but when you get in front of a crowd you always wow them. You have a strong work ethic and never mind putting in extra effort to get the job done. Your friends and family always know that they can count on you to help out if they are in a tight spot, which really makes them appreciate you!

If you chose mostly E's then you are most like Selena herself! A bubbly sweetheart with tons of energy, you are always fun to be with. You have lots of different types of friends and can bounce from group to group easily. You love doing high energy sports like surfing and skateboarding, but you also love chilling out to watch movies with your best buds. You are talented and smart and a very hard worker. You friends always come to you for advice because you are so level headed and you avoid drama, so they know their secrets are safe with you!

Would you and Selena be BFFs?

You are a big Selena fan, but would you and she hit it off? Take the quiz below to find out if you and Selena have what it takes to be best buds!

1. At the beach, you can be found:

    a. making a sandcastle and flirting with cute boys

    b. lounging in the sun with a good book

    c. surfing

2. You are throwing a big party for your birthday. What's the most important thing to you?

    a. that there is a big dance floor and rockin' music

    b. That all of you different groups of friends get along and have fun

    c. That there are plenty of snacks!

3. You best friend just got dumped. To cheer her up you:

    a. Crack jokes about her ex to make her laugh

    b. Make her Rice Krispie Treats and let her cry it out

c. challenge her to a basketball game to help her get her

   anger out on the court

4. For a Saturday night with friends you plan:

   a. a trip to the local karaoke bar to belt out all your favorite

      songs

   b. a movie night with lots of yummy snacks

   c. a trip to the skate park to show off your moves and hang

      out

5. For the school dance you wear:

   a. a brightly colored, girly dress that really stands out

   b. a simple dress with shoes you can dance in

   c. a skirt and top with brightly colored Converse sneakers

Now count up your answers and see if you and Sel could be friends forever!

If you chose mostly A's, then you love the spotlight — just like Selena. You are funny and talented. Selena loves to laugh and has a real flair for comedy so you two would make an unstoppable duo. You would have a blast cracking each other up! Plus you'd always be the life of every party with your silly antics.

If you chose mostly B's, then you and Selena would totally bond over your laid back ways. You both hate drama, so you like to keep things simple. You are always honest with your friends and are there to support them, but you don't get overly involved in their problems. You would be the go-to pair for advice and hanging out!

If you chose mostly C's then you and sporty Selena would totally get along. You both love playing sports — especially basketball, surfing, and skateboarding. But you have a girly side too and so does Selena. So you would have a lot of fun together hanging with your guy friends *and* going out shopping together!

Now that you've taken these super fun quizzes, share them with your friends. Chances are they are Selena fans who will love them just as much as you!